George

A GENTLEMAN OF THE ROAD

BY

P.A. DAVIES

First published as a paperback in 2013 by MJD Publishing, 920 Hyde Road, Manchester, M18 7LL, UK.

Email: mjdpublishing@gmail.com

ISBN: 978-0-9572639-1-8

First published as an e-book in 2013 by MJD Publishing.

ISBN (E-Book version): 978-0-9572639-2-5

Cover designed by Paul Anthony Davies.

Vagabond illustration designed by James Simpson.

Though certain events captured throughout this book are based on actual fact, the names and circumstances of some of the characters portrayed are of a purely fictional nature and not intended to represent any person or persons whether living or dead. Likewise, the views expressed by certain characters throughout the novel are again, written within a fictional context and are not intended to offend any person nor do these portrait the views of the author or any other persons.

"In a world full of imagination, anything is possible!"

P.A.Davies.

MY HEARTFELT THANKS TO:

All those people who have again, given me their valuable input in one way or another whilst I have been writing this novel … your feedback, unpaid proof reading and genuine interest have been warmly and gratefully received.

To Cath Watson for her unfaltering enthusiasm and support … a true friend indeed!

To James '*Square Pants*' Simpson for giving up his valuable time to read the finished manuscript and for the design of the Vagabond clip art!

And finally … to my daughter Maddison, just for being a part of my life x

****

1

I have to admit that it was a beautifully crafted one liner. A superbly delivered comeback that had the instant effect of making the recipient, look and feel like a complete fool. It wasn't rehearsed, it wasn't staged but my God, it couldn't have been scripted any better. In truth, the only downside that I could see with such a perfectly timed rebuff was the fact that I was the one on the receiving end of it.

15th July 2008. That's when it happened and it's a day that I certainly won't forget in a hurry. It was a day that had started out perfectly. A cloudless blue sky, a light warm breeze and a perfectly blended cappuccino sitting before me as I relaxed, al fresco, at a trendy city centre Bistro. This was my time. A couple of days off work, no pressing commitments and a copy of a new Jeffrey Archer novel to lose myself in for as long as I chose. Bliss!

And then I saw him, not more than one hundred feet from where I was sitting. Slowly but surely ambling towards me, occasionally stopping to invade the personal space of people sat outside other cafes, no doubt in the hope of a monetary gift. I shook my head and cursed under my breath knowing that this dirty looking man with unkempt grey hair, a wildly bushy beard and worn, filthy clothes would soon be standing next to me. And then, I suspected, he would give me that lost sheep look whilst holding out his grubby little hand or half eaten polystyrene cup that he'd dragged out of a stinking litter bin, expecting me to part with my hard earned cash. Well no way Jose! It was my money and he wasn't getting any of it. What he ought to do is get a job like the rest of us and stop scrounging off the good natured people trying to enjoy their lunch on one of the few sunny days that Britain rarely got in the height of the summer. Now sod off loser!

It was just a pity that, in reality, I wouldn't have had the heart to vocalise my thoughts or respond with a firm 'no!' and so had to think of a plan that would negate him pestering me into submission. It didn't help that I was sitting near to the footpath and would be within a mere two feet of Mr Scruffy's catchment zone as he passed. So, my plan needed to show all the cunning and guile of a confidence trickster yet be subtle enough not to cause too much offence. Above all, it needed to be bloody quick as he was now less than ten feet away.

And then it came to me in a blinding flash of clarity, as if it was the most obvious and most sensible choice in the world ... use the old German! Now, when I say the old German, I don't mean that I actually had an aged native of Germany sat with me, I meant use the language, or to be more precise, the one and only phrase that I knew ..."Ich spreche kein Englisch," ... which basically translates as, "I do not speak any English!" 'Perfect,' I thought. It was polite, it was quick and if used with a small shrug of the shoulders together with a vacant expression, it would surely encourage Mr Scruffy to move swiftly on. Ha! Fool proof!

I noticed that the first person he approached within our cordoned sanctuary, crumbled within seconds, handing over some coinage with a sympathetic smile. "Sucker," I muttered to myself as I watched the tramp move onto his next victim. The second person adopted the *totally ignore him and he'll go away* routine. This seemed a little too rude and cold for my liking but nonetheless, it worked a treat and forced him to move onto target number three. That particular person, the one closest to me, gave in as easily as target number one and duly handed over money that I saw amounted to about two pounds. '*Jesus*,' I thought with a touch of envy. '*He's made about three pounds in less than a minute!*'... And then, it was my turn.

As he bumbled towards me, I decided not to make eye contact but keep him well within my peripheral vision whilst pretending to read, ready to deliver my well rehearsed line immediately at the point where his hand reached out in hope. For some reason I was strangely nervous as if I was about to walk the boards in the leading role of a West End play. I could feel my heart pounding in my chest. I quickly went over the line in my head to make sure that I could actually say it with faultless conviction and convince the man that I was indeed a confused foreigner who couldn't speak a word of the Queen's. And before I knew it, there he was, standing next to me, hand outstretched and mumbling something that I truly didn't comprehend. This was it, the cue to say my piece, shrug the shoulders and watch a broken and deflated Mr Scruffy slope off to some other unwitting candidate, thus leaving me to enjoy the rest of my day in peace. Thank you and good afternoon!

I turned slowly, looking firstly at his hand and then up towards his face which I saw had been weathered by the outdoor elements. His beard was a yellowy grey colour and matted with remnants of old food that he had no doubt foraged from bins and skips around the city's streets. His thick hair, of similar shade and condition, seemed entwined with his facial hair and gave him the surreal appearance of a character from Lloyd Webber's *Cats*. What struck me the most though were his incredibly blue eyes. They were kind and warm yet looked like they had been taken from the head of a much younger man and placed into the leather clad sockets of his own. For just a split second I felt myself inexplicably weaken, wanting to do away with the whole charade, reach into my pocket and give the man some money. But no, I had to be strong and with the best German accent that I could muster, hit him with the killer line.

"Ich spreche kein Englisch," I said firmly with a shrug of the shoulders and even added a small apologetic smile for greater effect. The deed was done. Now all that remained was for the man to accept the rejection, walk away and leave me to revel in my success. Easy!

So why, when I had clearly spoken to him in German and announced that I couldn't speak English wasn't he leaving? And why the hell was he staring at me with those deep blue eyes and a faint smile on his lips? The reason was simple and quite frankly, enough to reduce me to about three feet in height. Holding me in his stare and speaking with a thick Scottish drawl, the man that I had pre-judged, yet clearly underestimated, merely replied. "That's ok son, neither dae Ah!"

And that was that. Point made. He gave a me a pitiful wink before sauntering off, leaving me in a wake of shame whilst he endeavoured to collect more hand-outs from the less tight arsed members of the public. Open mouthed, speechless and clearly feeling like an idiot, I shifted uneasily in my seat, not daring to look around at the other patrons for fear that they were looking right back at me, pointing and laughing. The man had clearly played me at my own game and won. By rights, I should have felt some antipathy for the man but as I watched him walk away, I couldn't help but feel a certain amount of respect and, if truth be known, a little humility. Here was I, sat in my own comfy world of self indulgence whilst a dishevelled looking Scot was traipsing around the city probably wondering where his next discarded box of half eaten KFC was coming from. And the more I thought about it, the more I wondered why he was living, nay existing, like he was and what had caused him to become a vagrant? Was it through unforeseen and unchangeable circumstances or was his a destiny of choice? Ordinarily I wouldn't have cared less. The world's full of tramps, so what? But something about this man intrigued me and I found myself inexplicably wanting to know more.

The next thing I know, I had approached Mr Scruffy and in a surreal turn of events, asked if he would consider telling me his life story. He stayed silent for a while, studying me through intensely suspicious eyes, scratching his chin beneath the thick layer of tangled beard as if in deep thought. I guessed he was thinking that I was perhaps a little mad. After all, it couldn't have been every day that he was asked to divulge his memoirs. I'd guessed wrong and for the second time that day, felt as though stupidity was my greatest virtue.

"Ah see your English has improved!" he said sardonically, raising a reproachful eyebrow.

Bloody hell! In my eagerness to find a story I'd completely forgotten that I was supposed to be a German bloke. What could I possibly say to that? As though sensing my obvious embarrassment and no doubt another victory, the man spared me my explanations as he continued.

"You're no' the Police are ye?" The word Police being pronounced as Po-lis.

"No," I snorted, a bit like a child who's denying eating all the biscuits despite having tell-tale crumbs all over his jumper. He looked at me with a little more suspicion, holding me in his stare as though considering his options ... or my intentions.

"Tell ye what," he eventually continued. "Call it fifty quid and a bottle o' single malt and ye can ask me what ye like!"

'Jesus,' I thought. 'When did the tramp become a Highway Robber. At least Dick Turpin wore a mask!' I considered haggling for a moment but deep down, knew that it wouldn't have made the slightest bit of difference ... not with a

Scot anyway! "Done," I said with overt enthusiasm, trying to make it sound like it was a bargain. I offered out my hand to him, which was an action that I regretted the second he took hold of it with his own dirt encrusted, five-digit shovel.

"Ye huv been!" he replied with a smile, whilst his vice like grip was in danger of stopping the circulation in my fingers.

"I'd have paid more!" I laughingly lied, hoping to gain the upper hand.

"And Ah'd huv taken a lot less!" he responded, sweeping the advantage from my grasp with effortless ease and a slight grin.

Surprisingly, I wanted to get down to the *interview* right there and then but in this crazy scenario, it transpired that the Scot had a prior engagement. Bizarre! What prior engagement could a tramp possibly have? Certainly not a high-powered business meeting with his accountant I mused. Nevertheless, I conceded unreservedly, suggested a day and time to meet up and even agreed to pay the requested retainer of ten pounds. "Just tae cover ma expenses," he said without flinching. I couldn't help but laugh as I handed over the money and though any normal onlooker might have suggested that I could kiss my hard earned cash goodbye, I had absolutely no doubt that this man would be at the agreed meeting place at the agreed time. And why was I so confident about this? Well, not because I trusted him particularly but because on this rapidly growing stage of oddities, the strangely interesting Mr Scruffy actually produced a small pocket sized diary from within his torn and dirty coat and wrote our appointment in it. I shook my head in disbelief and chuckled slightly. "What?" he asked firmly, whilst returning the diary to his coat. "Do ye no' think Ah huv a schedule too?" I treated this as a rhetorical question as I honestly didn't have a clue how to answer, especially as he had just scribed our engagement in a diary dated 1998. The man was either mad or genius but it wouldn't be until a few weeks later that I would learn the answer to that question.

And so it was that we had arranged to meet the following day. Twelve noon at his *office*. Piccadilly Gardens, Manchester ... a small area of public greenery in the midst of an otherwise concrete filled city. As he turned to walk away for a second time, a burning question suddenly popped into my head, a question that really needed answering for my own peace of mind. "By the way," I called after him. "How did you know that I wasn't a foreigner?" He looked at me and smiled, shaking his head slightly before revealing how his powers of observation had not failed him.

"Ah found it hard tae believe," he replied, still smiling. "That a true citizen of Germany would be reading an English copy of a Jeffrey Archer novel!"

2

The day couldn't have been any more different to that of its gloriously warm predecessor less than twenty four hours earlier and I began to wonder if, on a day this inclement, the man would even turn up for our little rendezvous in Piccadilly Gardens. It was wet and cold and grey. '*Not a day that would inspire anybody to sit down and recount their bygone days to a total stranger!*' I thought sombrely, as I looked in and around the bustling lunchtime crowd trying to spot him. Ten minutes passed, followed by another ten, followed by another and still he was nowhere to be seen. When forty-five minutes had slipped past our arranged meeting time, I'd lost faith that he would actually show and decided to call it a day. I couldn't help but curse myself for being so stupid and gullible enough to be taken in by some withered old git from Scotland. What was I thinking? Was I so naive to imagine that he would even remember me, let alone our appointment? I was duly vexed, I can tell you. And it cost me a tenner! Maybe I should have just ignored him in the first place, like any other normal self-respecting and disgusted taxpayer would have done. Or maybe I should have just gargled the contents of my coffee cup in his presence, proclaimed how utterly delicious it tasted and waved him on with a dismissive flick of the hand. Bastard!

But then, like a scene from some Biblical epic, the choppy sea of grey and sodden people suddenly parted, revealing the familiar figure of my scruffy new acquaintance, sat no more than one hundred feet from where I was standing. Now, I must admit that I was a tad relieved to see him and actually felt a little guilty for doubting his word. In truth, I wasn't expecting it to be that hard to spot such a distinctive looking homeless person in a relatively small area, but there again, I wasn't expecting him to be sat under a bright blue polka dot umbrella either.

"Nice brolly," I offered once I was stood by his side. "Selfridges?" I added in jest. He looked up at me with a scowl, clearly not amused by my little quip.

"There are two basic things that a man should always possess in life," he said rather sternly. "Honesty and punctuality!" I frowned as he continued. "Yesterdays performance aside, let's hope that ye are at least an honest man!"

'Hang on,' I thought. 'Is he having a go at me here or what? I think he's having a go!' I opened my mouth wanting to protest and tell him that, actually, I was here forty-five minutes earlier trying to find him but he quickly cut in as if sensing my sudden angst.

"Nae bother," he said standing up and closing his umbrella. "Yer here now, so let's forget it ever happened and start a fresh!" I was still open mouthed and slightly dumbfounded as he turned and gestured towards the far side of the gardens. "There's a wee cafe over there that does a crackin' one pound special at lunchtime!" He turned to me and asked. "Dae ye fancy it?" I could only shrug as he added. "It's on me?" No doubt his idea of a little sweetener.

"Fine," I managed, as he about turned and started to walk off in the direction of the bus station. I could hardly believe it. One minute I was quiet excited by the thought of listening to this old man's stories, the next, I was feeling like a child who had just been told off by his father. The thing was, I wasn't a child and he wasn't my dad. I'm in my forties for God's sake and he ... well ... he's just a scruffy down and out with a woman's polka dot brolly!

So why the hell did I feel so bad and why did I want to rush up to him and apologise profusely? I found myself wondering if now would be a good time to cut my losses and leave. I knew that I wasn't in the wrong and my God, how dare he speak down to me like that! On the other hand, maybe he needed telling about his attitude and you know what? That's exactly what I intended to do.

"Are ye coming or no'?" the man demanded, suddenly turning round. "It'll be closed at this rate!"

Jesus! ...There it was again ... Subtle, but another reprimand nonetheless. I stared at him for a few moments longer, mentally transmitting my annoyance in the hope that he would sense my pending wrath. I planned to put him straight on a few matters, believe me. But alas, whilst the plan of rebuking this man sounded like a real winner in my own mind, in reality, it probably would have worked better if my body and the rest of my brain were on board. As it turned out, all I could manage was to point at him like a cheesy American Game Show Host, give him a pathetic little wink and reply, "Right behind you my good man!"

Why I did this, I honestly couldn't tell you. Maybe it was just the old *respect your elders* teaching that I'd been brought up with or maybe I was harbouring some deep seated, subconscious fear that by speaking my mind, he would have actually removed his belt and tanned my backside for giving cheek. I really had no idea. But there it was, the final score in a game of emotional football. Scottish assertion one, English reproach, nil! Hurrah!!

When I finally sat down with my subject ... in one of the worst cafes I have ever entered in my life incidentally ... I noticed something a little different about the man, something that I couldn't quite put my finger on. He still had the same grubby look as he did the day before but something had definitely changed, apart of course from the introduction of the umbrella. And then it suddenly struck me what it was, causing me to chuckle slightly. My sudden outburst must have bemused him a little as he immediately stopped drinking his copper coloured tea mid loud slurp and looked over the rim of his oversized mug towards me, frowning. "Is there a problem?" he asked quietly as he put the cup down to reveal a tea soaked moustache.

"No, sorry!" I quickly replied. "It's just ... No, it doesn't matter, it's nothing, sorry!"

"It cannae be nothing," he added, his bright blue eyes seemingly probing my mind. "Unless ye huv t'retts syndrome that is?"

I shifted uneasily in my chair knowing that he wasn't going to let the matter drop, not until he had heard the excuse for my unexpected mirth. "Well," I began a little nervously. "I can't say that I've ever seen a tra ... a gentleman of the road ... wearing one of those before!" I nodded towards the area of his throat, causing him to reach up and touch the perfectly bound Windsor knot of his tie.

"Is it no' straight?" he asked with a slight, yet unfamiliar tone of worry in his voice.

"No, I mean, yes. It's fine. Very smart," I quickly added. "Just something I didn't expect to see that's all!"

The man nodded, though he still seemed a little tense. "But does it look ok though? It's no' too much is it?"

Extraordinary. Here I was, sat in a greasy spoon cafe, drinking a strange tasting brown liquid from a chipped blue mug, with a bloody tramp asking me about his dress sense. Surely life doesn't get any weirder. "It's spot on," I replied, the little white lie masked by my overt enthusiasm. "Red's obviously your colour!" Too far. The slightly embarrassed look on his face and the small bow of the head, confirmed this to me and then I felt really bad. Two nil to Scotland. He turned and gazed out of the window into a city that was benefitting from a fresh downpour of rain.

"Aye well," he said quietly. "If a man cannae make an effort on his wedding anniversary, then when can he?"

"What?" I exclaimed with genuine surprise. "You're married?"

"Was," he replied softly, still watching the rain. "It would've been sixty years today," he added and retouched his tie, smiling a little. After a moments silence, he suddenly turned back round to face me, frowning again. "And why are ye so surprised that Ah was married?" he asked directly, though I really didn't have a plausible answer to give him. "Ah'll tell ye this wee man," he continued with a lighter tone, sparing my non-existent opinion. "Ah was a hell of a catch in ma day y'know? Och aye. Ah had lassies flockin' fae all over the place Ah did!" He laughed a short but hearty laugh before picking up his mug and downing what was left of his tea.

"Do you fancy another?" I asked, sensing that neither of us wanted to go back out into the rain anytime soon.

"Would ye be treatin' me tae wan o' they scones too?" he asked devilishly.

"Only if you promise to tell me about your wife?" I offered, smiling. He looked at me with a half smile, half

11

grimace and I could see that, whatever the story was behind his wife or ex wife, he was obviously harbouring a great sadness that even *his* eyes couldn't hide. "If you want to that is?" I added, not wanting to push him and offering him a get out clause.

"Nae problem," he replied quietly. "But it's probably best we start at the beginning. Is that no' what ye wanted?"

"Och aye the noo!" I replied keenly in the best Scottish accent I could muster as I stood up. The man simply shook his head and raised his eyes to the ceiling.

"Jesus," he said in dismay. "And here was Ah thinking that your German accent was as bad as it gets!"

I laughed as I went to buy the tea and scones. '*Afternoon tea with a tramp*,' I suddenly thought with humorous disbelief. '*Maybe life does get weirder after all*!'

3

George Alexander Bell (the Alexander bit being after the great physician and inventor of the telephone, apparently) was born in Glasgow on February 29th 1928. A leap year no less.

"Hang on," I said with sudden surprise. "That would make you eighty years old!"

"Aye," George replied with a smile. "But only twenty in leap years!"

"I have to say George, you're looking well for eighty!" I added, genuinely. Despite his grey locks and facial hair, I personally would have put the man at no more than sixty years old. "It seems that street life is treating you well!"

"It has its moments," he said, devouring his scone as if he feared it would be taken back off him. Crumbs fell indiscriminately onto his beard and into his mug of tea, the former of which he casually swept onto the floor, the latter he drank as though it were an unforeseen bonus. "Maybe ye should try it," he added, through half masticated cake.

"Maybe I will," I began, sarcastically. "I can't imagine anything better than being sat in such a desirable eatery like this one after a hard days bin searching ... what joy!"

"Well yer sat here now aren't ye?" he asked, before slurping another mouthful of tea. I frowned then recoiled my head slightly. What could I possibly say in response to that mode of strange logic?

"Anyway," I began, quickly changing the path of conversation. "What was it like growing up in Glasgow in those days?" He sighed and sat back in his chair as if contemplating the question.

"A damn sight harder than being on the road, Ah can tell ye!" And that's exactly what he did.

It all started with George's great, great grandparents, Patrick and Katherine O'Leary, who left their beloved Ireland in the summer of 1847, to find work in Glasgow. Life had become incredibly hard in Ireland during that time, with the great potato famine seeing people lose their income, their homes and even their lives. So, the prospect of paid employment in a growing city such as Glasgow, was reason enough for the O'Leary's to pack up what few belongings they had and head for Scotland with their one and only child ... George's great grandma Mary, aged two.

George's great, great grandparents begged, borrowed and stole their way to the East coast of Ireland where they were lucky enough to board an empty coal ship bound for the coast of Scotland. It seemed that rides were given for free on those dirt-ridden vessels, as the passengers acted as human ballast, thus keeping the ship steady through rough seas.

13

"Jesus!" I exclaimed. "And that was classed as being lucky?"

"It was a far better option than the alternative!" George replied, leaning forward slightly and lowering his voice to a near whisper. "Coffin ships!" he added, as though the very mention of them was a sin against God. The fact that he quickly made the sign of the cross as he sat back in his chair, reinforced that this was perhaps a taboo subject, a subject that really shouldn't have been broached as to do so could bring about a thousand woes.

I thought about the implications of pursuing the topic of *Coffin Ships* and for some strange reason, felt a little wary, like I would be eternally hexed for showing the slightest interest. '*Probably best to leave it*,' I thought. '*It's obviously spooked George!*' I watched as the man loudly slurped his tea again in that ever so endearing way. Oh, what the Hell ... caution to the wind and all that!

"What were Coffin Ships George?" I asked, causing George to splutter into his tea. He removed the mug from his lips, placed it onto the table and wiped his beard with his sleeve. Class.

"Vessels of the Devil himself!" he exclaimed dramatically, waving a dismissive hand. "And no' a subject Ah feel totally comfortable wi'!"

Now I was really intrigued. Obviously, this needed a tactful approach if I was going to get the old man to talk about it. "Ok, George. It doesn't matter," I falsely stated. "Maybe I can read about it on the internet later!"

"What?" he quickly replied. "An' read a load o' nonsense written by somebody who wisnae even there?"

Hook.

"But neither were you!"

"Aye," he started defensively. "But at least Ah hud blood relatives who were there at that time!"

Line.

14

"I know, but I don't want to bother you and it's ..."

"What bothers me," George interrupted. "Is that ye would believe a load o' that internet tosh composed by some spotty twenty year old!" He paused for a moment. "Naw, naw," he continued. "If ye really want tae know, then it's best ye hear it from somebody who actually knows what they're talkin' aboot!"

And sinker ... Reel him in my good man.

George told me about the coffin ships and how thousands of Irish men, women and children sought to board them; mainly as a result of false hope given out by unscrupulous landlords determined to get tenants off their land at the height of the great potato famine. They were fed lies about the great opportunities awaiting them in North America and how both food and work were plentiful. Added to this, firm promises were made that any family willing to take this option, would automatically qualify to receive money and accommodation on arrival in America. Some families were even given the fare towards the cost of travel as an added incentive to leave the land. "Can ye imagine how they must've felt?" George asked. "One minute they wur wondering how they would feed themselves, the next they wur being told aboot this new and exciting life to be hud in America!"

"They must have been ecstatic," I replied. "But surely they knew that it sounded too good to be true?"

"Maybe, maybe no'," he replied. "But if you and yer family were starvin' tae death and somebody offered ye this golden ticket, would ye no' want tae believe it was true?" I couldn't help but think that yes, I probably would. "And that," he continued. "Was all the incentive that thousands of down-trodden, hard working Irish men and women needed to make them rush, like lemmings, to the sea ports and board the most unseaworthy, disease ridden ships known to man!" Another pause to slurp his tea. "They were crammed intae those ships like sardines in a can. Ships that hud poor sanitation, little food and water and would huv sunk faster than a lead weight if they ever hit bad weather, which happened many times, believe me. Fever, starvation, the occasional suicide by distraught souls who hud lost their whole family tae any of the above and of course, murder!" He must have seen the look of surprise on my face. "Oh aye!" he confirmed. "It wisnae unusual for single men to huv their throats cut whilst they slept and their food rations taken by men with their own starving families to feed. It was survival son, pure and simple. And then there was typhus, a disease that spread like wild fire and claimed the lives of countless men, women and children. All these were the norm son, no' the exception and on a journey that lasted several weeks in the most vile conditions, it was a lottery tae see if ye would actually reach America alive!" He paused again, shook his head and let out a sigh. "It's said that sharks used tae follow the coffin ships knowing that sooner or later, corpses would be thrown over board in their dozens? Whether that's true or no' Ah couldnae say. But what Ah dae know is that thirty per cent o' the people who boarded those ships in search o' a better world, never made it across the Atlantic!"

"Thirty per cent!" I repeated in amazement. "That's a hell of a lot of people to lose their lives just by taking a boat journey!"

"Which is why they called them coffin ships son. And here's something else ye might like to know!" He leaned forward again and lowered his voice slightly for full effect. "The ghosts of those who perished at sea during those terrible journeys, still haunt the waves of the Atlantic tae this very day!"

"What?" I replied with a tone of outward cynicism. "As in real ghosts?" I gave him a disbelieving and (quite frankly) a mildly patronising look, which he met with a disapproving scowl.

"Ye might scoff yer ignorance," he retorted bluntly. "But the sight o' deed Mothers wailing for their lost babies and young men crying out for help when they donae even know they huv passed on, is enough to chill even the hardest o' souls!"

"Well, I don't believe in ghosts," I added dismissively. "Or old wives tales for that matter!"

"An' Ah would agree," he quietly concurred.

'Right then,' I thought. *'So what's with the attitude?'*

"Had Ah no' seen them with ma own eyes!"

'Fair enough!'

He looked out of the window and appeared to go off into a distant world of his own, whilst I sat there open mouthed, gawping at him like a fool. Did I just hear right? Did he actually say that he had seen the ghosts of some unfortunate Irish citizens that had died over one hundred and sixty years ago? Had he been privy to a haunting spectacle that I thought only existed in the writings of Stephen King? ... Bollocks! "So," I began to quiz. "You've actually seen ghosts floating around the Atlantic Ocean?" He came out of his temporary daydream and looked at me with a slight frown.

"D' ye think Ah'm lyin' son?" he asked, as if he couldn't believe that I had actually questioned the authenticity of his statement.

'Hell yes!' I wanted to shout out. *'There's no such things as ghosts my good man!'* "No of course not," is what I actually replied. "But ... well ... ghosts? It's a bit hard to take in, you know? Especially for a non believer like me!"

"Aye, that's true enough," he agreed. "And nothing or naebody would huv convinced me that they existed either. No' until that day that is!" He looked down at his wrist as if wanting to check the time and then sighed as though he had only just realised that he didn't actually own a watch! "What time is it now?" he asked, with a slight sense of urgency in his voice.

I checked, and then re-checked the position of the hands on my own watch. "Jesus!" I answered, with some surprise, "It's quarter past four already. Where the hell has the afternoon gone?" George rose quickly from his seat. "Where are you going?" I asked hastily in some crazy parental tone reserved only for children who needed to seek permission to leave the table. The raising of a rebuttal eyebrow from the man put me back in my place. "Sorry George," I added sincerely. "But I thought you were going to tell me about *that day*? Y'know? When you saw the ghosts?"

"Tae be honest," he sighed. "It's no' a subject Ah like tae talk aboot too much!"

'*For fifty quid and a bottle of Scotch, you'd better get to like it George old boy!*' I thought bitterly.

"But Ah suppose yer paying me," he added, as if reading my mind. Christ! How does he do that? "Although it will huv tae be another day," he continued, bizarrely checking his invisible watch again. "Ah huv tae be somewhere else just now!"

'*Where the hell does a tramp have to be?*' I thought with equal bitterness. '*This is the second time he's done this!*' "Ok," I quietly conceded as I rose from my chair. "When can we meet up again then?" I was very eager to hear the rest of his ghostly story.

"Call me," he said with convincing seriousness and then began to chuckle, no doubt from the look of pure astonishment on my face, as I momentarily believed that he actually owned a mobile phone.

"Very funny," I replied sardonically, though secretly admitted that it was a little bit comical, even if the joke was at my expense ... again!

We agreed to meet at the same time, same place the following week and although I would have liked it to have been the following day, I had learnt (even in the short time I had known him) that George was not a man to compromise whatever schedule he normally adhered to. Patience isn't my strongest virtue and I really didn't relish the idea of having to wait a full week to hear the rest of his life story. What I didn't know at that point, but can tell you now, was that his would be a story well worth waiting for.

4

To George, it had seemed like a good idea at the time, especially as he didn't relish the idea of National Service. He had failed to see why he should offer his *services* involuntarily to a nation that had offered practically nothing to his family pre World War two and even less during it. So, in the March of 1946, having turned eighteen the month before, he figured that the best way to avoid the *draft,* was to join the crew of a fishing trawler bound for the Atlantic Ocean. And that's exactly what he did.

As the aged, fifty foot vessel chugged out of the dock on that unseasonably mild morning, George stood to the rear of the boat watching the silhouetted buildings of the fishing port become smaller and smaller until they finally faded into the backdrop of the rugged and imposing hills of the coastline. Seagulls relentlessly voiced their high-pitched cries as they followed in the wake of the trawler, eager to have their fill of bait or the contents of disembowelled fish thrown overboard by the crew. George watched as they soared effortlessly above him, their white and grey bodies barely visible against the deep purple and crimson hues of the early morning sky. What he found strangely sensational was that to the front of the boat, he could still see the stars, shining like crystals against a blanket of darkness, whilst behind it, the tentacles of a heavenly radiance reached out from the land, as night was gently eroded by the start of a new day. The rising sun cast an eerie glow across the calm surface of the sea, giving it the appearance of a deep red wine, occasionally splintered by the white foaming summits of breaking waves. It seemed like a million miles away from the depressing grey of inner City Glasgow. George smiled as a fresh breeze swept over him, his face gently moistened by the salty spray of the sea. '*This*,' he thought, '*is by far, the best decision Ah huv ever made!*' It was the first time he had ever left good old terra firma, but if initial impressions were anything to go by, it certainly wouldn't be his last. What's more, he had victoriously evaded marching around some stupid Army parade ground being shouted at by some loud-mouthed bully of a Sergeant Major, who would have him doing everything at double time, just because he could. No, no. That wasn't for George. '*A life on the ocean waves*,' he thought contently. '*Catching fish and listening to the old hands recalling interesting stories whilst smoking on their pipes and drinking rum. And nae loud mouth soldier to bark shi ...*'

"Those fuckin' nets wullnae ready their sels George!" a voice suddenly boomed from behind him, making him jump and re-enter reality at a remarkable pace. He quickly turned around and saw the Captain glaring at him. George's mouth fell open as he stood nervously before a man that he had heard his mother speak of many times before and from the accurate description given, recognised immediately. The man's reputation was near legendary, though it was a legend that most people would rather hear about than have to face in person.

Isaac 'Armadillo' Andrews, trawler owner and part-time dock fighter. A squat man whose thickset, unshaven jawline reminded George of Desperate Dan from The Dandy Comic, a similarity that he wasn't about to share openly. He had an old, deep scar running from the corner of his left eye to the bottom of his cheek, a legacy from one of his many bouts and a complexion that was the colour and texture of antique hide leather. His dark piercing eyes had the bizarre appearance of looking both eternally angry yet uncannily kind and George could only imagine what sights they had witnessed over the years to make them so. What Andrews lacked in height, he more than made up for in brawn, with his large barrel chest and shovel like hands earning him the endearing title that likened him to that small armour plated mammal with big claws. He wasn't a man renowned for his patience and was said to have a fuse shorter than the unlit cheroot that hung unceremoniously, yet traditionally, from his lips. If the Recruitment Clerk in the Harbour Masters office had bothered to mention whom the Captain of The Pearl of Good Hope actually was, George mused, he probably would have considered the Army parade square to be a far easier option.

"Noo get the shite cleared oot o' they nets, mop the decks an' prepare the bait!" he growled. "Ah want tae start making a living sometime the day and Ah've nae room for idle bastards aboard ma boat who cannae earn their supper, let alone their pay! D'ye hear me George?" George heard him all right and so did every other hand on the boat, judging by the amount of laughing that was going on.

###

I chuckled as George relayed the story, his facial expressions re-living every second of his encounter. "Sounds like he was a scary bloke," I offered genuinely.

"An' that's puttin' it mildly, Ah can tell ye!" George responded with great conviction. "Blood curdlin' would be more exact!"

I laughed again at the look of mild distress on the old man's face before adding. "So it wasn't quite what you expected then George?"

"No' at that point," he replied succinctly, shaking his head. "In fact, it only got worse the longer the trip went on!" George took a large bite from a bacon sandwich that a disinterested and uninspired teenage waitress had placed in front of him. He chewed it vigorously for a couple of moments then suddenly stopped, mid-chomp and frowned. He opened up the remaining sandwich for inspection, shook his head and reached for the Daddy's Brown Sauce. "It wisnae a complicated order, was it?" he muttered to himself, as if quietly chastising the world and all the bored waitresses who bothered to work in it. He smothered the pinky-brown, fatty meat with the sauce, re-constructed the sandwich and took another sizeable bite from it. This time, he hummed a tone of satisfaction as he chewed, before washing down the contents of his mouth with a large swig of copper coloured tea. He belched, (pleasant) and looked at me directly. "Bacon without brown sauce," he began in earnest. "Like a blunt pencil!"

"What?" I asked, with a quizzical frown.

"Y'know, a blunt pencil" he repeated. "Pointless!"

"Oh, right!"

"No' too quick on the uptake are ye son?" he scoffed.

"Oh, sorry George," I replied with some sarcasm and a little bitterness. "How stupid of me not to get the old *bacon butty and blunt pencil* analogy. What an utter arse I must be!"

"An' a little touchy tae!" he added with a wry smile.

Another point for the kilted nation.

"Anyway, where was Ah?"

"Captain Armadillo and the trawler from hell!" I prompted.

"Oh aye ... Isaac Andrews ... well!"

By 10am on 3rd March 1946, George was knackered. His arms ached, his back ached and he had blisters on his hands the size of shillings. Despite this, he couldn't help but crack a little smile at the result of all his hard graft. The deck was gleaming. Crates and lobster pots that were normally discarded haphazardly around the boat had been stacked with such enviable precision that even some of the crew had grunted their surprised approval. Captain Andrews looked on from the raised platform of his wheelhouse, quietly admiring George's handy-work. "Nice work George!" he called out to an exhausted looking eighteen year old. "Will ye be ready for some grub?"

"Aye Captain, Ah will that," George answered, feeling relieved to be getting a break at last. "Ah could eat a scabby pit horse!"

"Ah'm sure ye could," the Captain said laughing, though George sensed a distinct falseness in his mirth. "And as soon as the first catch is brought in and stored," Andrews continued. "Ye can fill your belly till it bursts!" George's heart sank. "But Ah cannae promise a pit horse Georgie boy, scabby or otherwise!" Again, the Captain and his crew laughed, but this time it was genuine ... and cutting. Had George had any energy left, the small spark of anger that he felt beginning to smoulder deep within, would have ignited into a full blown furnace of rage and sod the consequences. As it was, he could do little but bow his head in dismay and listen as Andrews shouted a command. "Pull 'em in boys and let's see what Poseidon has given us!" All hands went to the rear of the deck as the huge, diesel powered winch was fired up and set to pull a laden fishing net back towards the boat.

"Don't mind him George," one of the crew said quietly, gesturing towards the Captain. "He's jus' testin' the strength of yer mettle. Huv ye ever hauled a catch before?" George shook his head. "Well, stick wi' me and follow ma lead son," the man directed. "It's easier than it looks!"

A few hours later, the first catch of fresh fish had been pulled aboard, gutted, packed in crates and stored in the chilled darkness below the deck. George dripped with sweat and was saturated with the vile stench of fish innards, an odour that was making him feel extremely nauseous. In fact, it wasn't too long before he was rushing to the side of the boat to hurl what little he had in his stomach, into the sea, much to the amusement of the crew. "Welcome to sea trawlin' George," somebody called out, causing a ripple of laughter and applause amongst the men. George remained in situ for a good while longer, letting the sea air wash over him in a bid to ease his churning stomach. He suddenly felt a hand on his shoulder and when he turned around, was surprised to see the Captain stood behind him, holding out a battered looking metal cup.

"Here, drink this," he said. "It'll make ye feel better!" George wanted to ask what was in it and wondered if, as a practical joke, he was actually being given something that would make him feel worse. In truth, he was past caring and took the offering anyway. "Ye did alright laddie," was all that Andrews added, before walking away. A flabbergasted George looked at the crew and again, they began to applaud, only this time, it was born out of respect and acceptance for their newest recruit ... and George smiled.

"Near on three years Ah was a hand on that trawler," George said, looking out of the cafe window into a world that was miles away from what anybody else could see. After a few moments in his own thoughts, he came back to the present and turned back to me. "Made a man of me, Ah can tell ye!"

"I can imagine," I replied. "Though three years is a long time for somebody who didn't like it much. What made you stay?"

"Well, it wisnae long before Ah discovered that working for a man like Isaac Andrews, brought a certain amount of privileges," he replied. "An' Ah don't just mean a regular wage!" he added with a slight wink. I was intrigued and urged George to continue the story, though I sensed he didn't actually need any more encouragement from me. The man was on a roll.

###

Isaac Andrews

5

World War II brought about the introduction of Government imposed rationing to Great Britain. More worryingly to Isaac Andrews, is that it also brought about a significant slump in the fishing industry, as rumours of German U-Boats and sea mines taking out trawlers whilst they went about their business, drastically cut the hours spent harvesting the ocean stocks. The threat of being blown out of the water by some sneaky Nazi bastard, didn't really bother Isaac, though he found it incredibly difficult to find the same defiant attitude in any of his crew members, thus leaving him too short on hands to help man his vessel. As Isaac's age had negated him from the inevitable call-up to fight for King and Country against the *Gerry*, he quickly needed to find a side-line career to help subsidise his existence or face the prospect of a life less fortunate.

Using his connections with some of the more unsavoury and less scrupulous purveyors of Glasgow's expanding black market, Andrews began to solicit his menacing physical appearance amongst the numerous loan sharks of the city, offering out his services as a freelance debt collector. With an intimidating, no nonsense approach, it wasn't long before he had made his mark in the community and built up such a solid reputation amongst the backstreet financiers, that each and every one of them had started to offer him greater amounts of money in the hope of securing his expertise. For a while, times were good for Isaac, though ironically, it was his expertise that led to yet another slump in his earnings. Within two years of him starting out, the good citizens of Glasgow thought it wiser to pay their dues on time, rather than risk a personal visit from the *Mad Fisherman* and with the debtors now paying on time, the call for his services, together with his income, started to dwindle.

Enter Samuel O'Donnell, one of the city's more successful bookmakers who had hired Isaac on numerous occasions to assist in the collection of a few overdue betting accounts. O'Donnell had seen a substantial growth in a particular market and despite the risks to his reputation (and freedom), wanted in. It was a market not featured in any of the regular sporting columns nor backed by any official body, but it was a market that was undoubtedly set to yield a significant purse, especially if the odds were stacked in your favour. And in the case of the bookmaker, discreetly securing the services of Isaac Andrews to represent his interests in this ever expanding pastime, was a win-win situation. After all, not only was the man built like a brick outhouse, but he was also a bad tempered, ill mannered and stubborn animal; a perfect combination of the traits required for the world of bare knuckle fighting.

###

"Wow!" I interrupted excitedly. "So Isaac was an actual Street Fighter?"

"The best in Glasgow, by all accounts," George replied, with a slight tone of admiration. "An' from what Ah could gather, undefeated!"

"In how many fights?" I asked.

"Hard to tell," George replied. "Though Ah would say more than a hundred!"

"What?" I gasped. "One hundred fights?"

"At least," George replied. "He would huv two or three bouts a week apparently, though the only person who made any real money oot o' it, was the bookmaker himself. He would take the bets and set the odds and all the while, be quid's in, even if Isaac lost a fight, which he never did. Came close once though!"

George went on to tell me how one particular challenger had decided to turn up at a fight with a flick knife hidden in the waistband of his trousers. A little insurance policy against becoming another statistic of defeat. The fight had taken place in one of the wharfs many disused warehouses and had the makings of a real classic. Isaac's adversary was a huge Polish immigrant who had already made a substantial career out of fighting throughout the cities and towns of Scotland and who was also undefeated. He was a nasty individual, who often ignored the unwritten laws of bare knuckle fighting and had regularly continued to pummel his defeated opponents despite their cries of submission. He was actually seen as a liability to the *good name* of the illegal sport, as many feared that his actions would one day lead to the death of another. And that would be a right royal inconvenience.

However, Marek Slovoski, (as that was his name) was not a man to be reasoned with and there was nobody who would dare approach him to offer a friendly word of warning, not unless they wanted to find their throat at the mercy of his vice like grip that was. In truth, a contest that involved an appearance by Slovoski, would undoubtedly bring in huge crowds and therefore, huge wagers. And, as money speaks volumes in the Land of the Greedy, the small issue of his ungentlemanly conduct remained frowned upon, but never broached.

The warehouse was packed to capacity that night, with excited punters noisily placing their bets as they waited for the two men to enter the makeshift boxing ring and start their bout. Though the temperature outside the warehouse was well below freezing, the heat that radiated from over three hundred, highly charged spectators, was enough to make even the semi naked bodies of the fighters sweat. Low wattage bulbs struggled to illuminate the fighting area and could only offer a yellowy, grey triangle of haze above the ring. But this wasn't Madison Square Gardens, it was the docks of Glasgow and as long as the fighters could see each other and the crowd could see the fighters, then let the games begin.

The crowd roared their approval as each competitor entered the ring and though the Pole was seen as the favourite to win this particular meeting, the plaudits for both men remained equally rapturous. With the introductions and formalities over, the two men stood alone in the ring, staring intently at each other whilst waiting for the first bell to sound.

Isaac remained still and stony-faced, trying not to allow his deeply hidden but ever present nerves rise to the surface and show as a sign of weakness to his opponent.

Marek stretched his arms and clicked his neck muscles whilst all the time glaring at Isaac, with hate in his eyes and an evil grin fixed mockingly on his face.

To all in the venue, the Pole looked intimidating, fired up and confident that this pending clash was going to be a walk in the park. No more than a two rounder at most.

Isaac secretly wondered if he could actually beat the man stood before him or would he too, like so many other contenders, be pasted into the floor without mercy.

Unbeknown to Isaac and the baying crowd, Marek Slovoski was thinking exactly the same about the Scotsman.

In a prequel to the sounding of the first bell, the noise of the crowd became uncannily hushed, as though somebody had pushed an invisible mute button. The air was dense with anticipation and excitement, an atmosphere so highly charged, that it could almost be quantified by touch alone. The spectators waited with shallow patience, each and every one of them fixing a wide-eyed, unfaltering stare on the fighters whilst quietly urging the timekeeper to do his thing. And then, as the hammer finally connected with the metal casing of the large brass bell, the illusory volume control of the clamouring crowd was re-set to full.

Within only a few seconds of the fight starting, Isaac was shaking his head, trying desperately to clear it of the swimming haze as he sat, uncharacteristically, on the floor of the fighting ring. As his senses began to return, he looked up and saw the large frame of his opponent hovering above him with the slight frame of the referee attempting to push him back. In a bizarre mental interlude, Isaac thought that it looked quite comical, as though Mohammed was attempting to move the proverbial mountain ... and he smiled.

When the official eventually stood over the fallen fighter to begin his count, Isaac considered the only two options he had ... get up and return to the battle or stay down, be counted out and lose. He had not expected a man of Slovoski's size to move with such speed and had certainly not expected to be caught out with such a fearsome punch so early on.

"One ... two ... three ..."

If he were to get up, he would need to watch this man more carefully, find his weaknesses and avoid his strengths.

"Four ... five ... six ..."

But would that be enough or would he find himself on the seat of his pants again? His jaw ached like a bitch and he suspected it was probably broken. Feeling around the inside of his mouth with his tongue, he noticed a couple of loose teeth and could taste the familiar tang of blood mixed with saliva. He spat violently, causing one of the teeth to free itself from his injured gum and shoot out dramatically onto the floor in front of him.

"Seven ... eight ..."

Common sense was urging him to stay down. Accept defeat and avoid any further, unnecessary pain.

"Nine ..."

'*Bollocks to that!*' he thought defiantly and with a renewed holler of excitement from the crowd, rose to his feet before the count reached ten.

The Pole's grin faltered as he watched Isaac rise from the floor. He had hit him with what was probably one of his best shots yet incredibly, the man was getting back up. He felt sure that one more like-punch to Isaac's jaw would finish him off but he needed to act quickly; preferably whilst Isaac was still a bit muggy and disorientated but definitely whilst his line of sight was being temporarily blocked by the referee checking on his welfare ... Slovoski advanced.

The crowd saw Slovoski move in for the kill and noticeably gasped at the man's defiance of the sport's Code of Conduct. It was common knowledge to both competitors and onlookers, that a fight should only continue on the direction of the referee, not before and certainly not when he was checking on one of the fighters. But this was Marek Slovoski's trademark and the punters lapped it up, with a few even cheering him on.

As he neared Isaac's position, many predicted that the end was nigh for the fisherman and looked forward to collecting their winnings. What they didn't predict was the abnormally quick reaction of a man still partially stunned and the precision with which he moved. When the referee shifted slightly to one side, Isaac caught a fleeting glance of the Polish freight train heading towards him. And whilst it was just enough movement for Isaac to see Slovoski advancing, it was also little enough for Slovoski not to notice him looking. '*And there lies his weakness,*' Isaac quickly mused. '*Over confidence marred by stupidity!*'

Timing was the key. Timing and accuracy. Without those, the counter attack would have been no more than a mere inconvenience to the Pole, an inconvenience that he would have been both willing and able to rectify. But Isaac lacked neither timing nor accuracy and as Slovoski was within a whisper of his position, he acted with the grace and speed of an athlete who had youth on his side. He quickly and easily pushed the referee to one side and took a small step to his left, putting his stronger right arm in direct alignment with that of Slovoski's body. A look of astonished, grim understanding appeared on Marek's face and though he tried to slow his pace and change direction, it was way too late, as the momentum he had already established, kept his heavy build on the initial line of attack. Isaac bent his knees slightly, recoiled his arm and with unparalleled force and precision, released a punch that struck his opponent directly in the solar plexus. Marek not only stopped in his tracks, but also appeared to travel marginally backwards before doubling over with a pained growl. Isaac quickly sprang to the side of Slovoski and administered a further punch to his temple, sending him crashing to the floor. The crowd were ecstatic and though there were shouts of *"Finish him!"* that wasn't Isaac's style and he simply moved into a neutral corner as the referee started yet another count. The Pole was up in four and literally ran at Isaac with the temperament of a wounded animal: angry and vicious. He swung a haymaker at the Scot which, had it achieved full contact, would have literally taken Isaac's head clean off his shoulders. Fortunately, Isaac ducked just enough to avoid the full impact of the Pole's right fist but was unable to evade a quickly following, less powerful left, that struck him just above his ear. As Marek reset his position, Isaac countered with a shot to his kidneys before moving away. Slovoski gave chase and closed Isaac down and within a matter of seconds, the two were toe to toe, battling it out with an equal match of jabs and hooks. The volume in the room was such, that nobody heard the bell sounding the end of round one and the fight continued until the referee finally found the courage to place himself in between the men and break them up.

The following rounds were as intense as the first, with each fighter becoming as blooded and as bruised as the other. By the tenth round, it was pure and utter stubborn determination that was keeping the pair going, with every blow received or delivered now having little effect. Neither man was about to give up and the bout became locked in a stalemate. But it was Slovoski's actions that were to change all of that and bring an unexpected and sudden end to the fight.

Round eleven. And at the sound of the bell, Marek raced across to Isaac with surprising energy. He grabbed hold of the Scot and in a move typical of his reputation, head-butted Isaac, hard. There was loud crack as the bridge of Isaac's nose snapped like a dry twig and he fell, like a laden sack, onto all fours. A bloody grin appeared on Slovoski's face that gave him the look of a deranged psychopath about to kill without feeling or mercy. He swung his leg towards the groaning and disoriented Scot, catching him directly in the ribs. There was another sickening crack as bone fractured from the force of the blow, a crack that was audible even above the yelp of the disbelieving onlookers. Isaac rolled onto his back in excruciating pain whilst the referee attempted to have words with Marek about his unsavoury methods. The Pole growled at the official before picking him up and throwing him out of the ring like discarded litter.

"Out of order!" somebody shouted from the crowd, though Marek just laughed then roared at them, walking around the ring, tensing his gross physique in a show of egotistical superiority whilst Isaac lay still on the deck. The mood in the gathering of spectators changed, with a succession of loud and united disapproving boos being fired towards the battle scarred Polish giant.

"You vanted fight," Marek shouted in broken English. "I give you fight!"

"Then fight fairly y' bastard!" somebody shouted back.

"Maybe I fight you next?" Marek replied menacingly. "But first," he continued, turning towards Isaac. "I have unfinished business with veak fisherman!" Slovoski spat out a mixture of blood and phlegm before heading back over to Isaac. He stood over his adversary, sneering at the battered man now lay on his back panting, eyes partially shut from the excessive swelling around his sockets. "You lose!" he hissed, as he lifted his right leg and brought his foot down hard towards Isaac's skull.

"Ooo nasty," I said, grimacing and recoiling slightly at George's recount. "I bet that hurt. But I thought you said that Isaac never lost a fight?"

"And he never did," replied George, taking another slurp from his mug.

"What?" I quizzed, with a little confusion. "So, some big Pole stamps on Isaac's head and you're telling me that he wasn't finished?"

"What Ah'm telling ye, is no' what ye're hearing," George answered casually, sending me into a deeper state of bewilderment. George looked at me and smiled. "Did Ah, at any time, tell ye that Marek's foot made contact with Isaac's head?" he asked.

"Well," I replied, quickly recalling the story. "You told me that Slovoski brought his foot down, hard, towards Isaac's head, so I presumed that ..."

"There ye go," George cut in with a slight hoot and a tap of the table, as if a point of order had just been made.

"There you go what?" I asked, a bit shortly. Well ... I can't be doing with bloody riddles. Just get to the point for God's sake.

"Just like the crowd," George continued, with a small but noticeably irritating sigh. "Ye presumed that the foot had reach its intended target and that Isaac was lying there badly injured and defeated, yes?"

"Well, yes. But ..."

"Then, like the crowd," George cut in, yet again, "Ye underestimated the tenacity of this particular Scot!"

6

When Isaac had hit the ground for a second time, pain surged through his body like he had been pierced with a white hot, serrated knife and for the first time in his fighting career, he was ready to embrace the Referee's count. He had decided that enough was enough and would have been content to bow out gracefully whilst Marek Slovoski basked in the glory of a win ... but the count didn't come.

In the moments that followed his knockdown, Isaac heard the Pole prance about the ring with a cutting arrogance, goading the crowd and whipping them into a frenzy of varying emotions with his display. Anger, excitement, anticipation. It was the stuff that historical bare-knuckle fights were made of and the punters lapped it up. And it was in those few moments of distraction, that Isaac felt a sudden urge wash over him. An urge that would be foolish to follow, though impossible to ignore and he found himself unexpectedly warming to the idea of getting back up onto his feet and showing Mr Slovoski exactly why Scotland was so great. But to continue the battle,

Isaac would need to dig deep into his resources and he would need to do it quickly, as Slovoski's little side show was not going to last forever.

Through bruised and slatted eyes, he watched as Marek leant over the ropes of the ring and waved his fists at the crowd, spraying them with blood-infused spit as he viciously responded to their chants. As a seasoned gladiator in the arena of bare-knuckle bouts, Isaac had encountered many unorthodox fighters such as Slovoski and was in little doubt as to what the Pole's next move would be. But he also knew that, in order to counter it, he would need to stay sharp and act with the speed and accuracy that any other man finding themselves in his current position, would struggle to think about, let alone execute.

And then he saw Slovoski (with a more pressing matter to attend to) turn his back on the crowd, look across the ring and smile. With a noticeable sigh and a discharge of spit, he strolled towards Isaac and stood above him, cocking his head as if considering the most apt way to finish off his fallen prey.

Isaac felt the adrenaline pound through his body as Marek approached, rocketing the clarity of his senses to a high that even *he* didn't know existed. When Slovoski was stood over him, Isaac turned his head slightly towards the aggressor and immediately noticed him shift his line of balance. He knew what was coming and though he heard the Pole speak, he was too focused on his objective to respond to what was said.

Now, if there was an imaginary switch that could be used to sedate the current speed of life, then in Isaac's mind, somebody had just flicked it on. In a bizarre interlude of slow motion action, he watched as Slovoski raised his leg high and then begin to bring it down towards his head, a move that Isaac knew would put Marek's stability at a temporary disadvantage.

The crowd saw neither the slow motion action nor the impending disadvantage of Marek's position. What they did see was an incredibly fast, incredibly accurate and wholly unexpected manoeuvre by a man whom they had already written off as dead in the water. As Slovoski's foot was within three inches of its intended target, Isaac's hands flew up from his sides in a blur, grabbed the Pole's foot mid travel and held it in situ with undeniable strength. The audience gasped in awe whilst the conceited look on Marek's face quickly faded and changed to that of shocked dis-belief. He tried to pull his foot free from the vice like grip but this only served to unsteady him and cause him to hop on one leg as he attempted to regain his balance. The crowd laughed mockingly and then cheered, as Isaac twisted the foot so hard that Marek's ankle dislocated with a loud clunk, making the Pole shriek and fall backwards onto the seat of his pants. With newfound agility, Isaac was suddenly back on his feet, delivering a powerful kick between Slovoski's legs, a connection that even brought tears to the eyes of the onlookers.

"That's for ma broken rib!" Isaac growled, before delivering a further kick to the exact same target. "An' that's for dis-respectin' the Official!"

Outside the ring, looking in, the Referee knew that he should have been intervening at this point and putting a stop to Isaac's *unprofessional* conduct. But he only smiled and remained steadfast, quietly enjoying Marek's comeuppance. Only when Isaac had walked away from the battered Pole, did he climb back through the ropes and administer the count. This time he made it to ten and declared Isaac Andrews the winner, raising the fighter's arm to the cheers of an ecstatic crowd. All eyes were now firmly fixed on the undefeated Scot. So much so, that nobody noticed when Marek sat upright nor when he slowly got back to his feet and leant against the ropes, trying to regain his stability. It was only when he produced a slim black object from within the band of his trousers and pushed a small button on it, causing a four-inch blade of shining steel to flick out, that somebody finally noticed.

"Knife," a man shouted. "He's got a knife!"

All heads turned back to the Pole just in time to see him advancing towards Isaac, snarling loudly. For a second time that night, a stunned and pale looking Referee was pushed to one side as Marek bore down on Isaac. With the first vicious swing of the knife, the blade made contact with Isaac's left cheek, cutting deep into the tissue like a hot knife through butter and causing him to shout out in both pain and anger. Seeing a fresh stream of blood, Slovoski became like a man possessed, flailing the knife wildly at Isaac, hoping to inflict another wound. Though Isaac managed to dodge and weave away from most of Slovoski's numerous attempts, the second hit finally came, as Marek thrust the knife towards Isaac's chest and caught him directly on the left pectoral muscle. Whether it was an act of God, weakened steel or (as most had settled on and would talk about time and time again) the sheer *Armadillo-esque* hardness of Isaac's torso, nobody *actually* knew why the blade of the knife immediately split in half as it connected with the Fisherman's chest and left little more than a nick in his skin. Slovoski stared disbelievingly at Isaac's chest and then at the broken knife, now sporting a shattered, two-inch blade. When he looked up again, Isaac was already upon him, leaving him no time to react. Within seconds, Isaac had gripped the Pole's knife wielding hand and twisted it so hard and fast that the wrist snapped with ease. And then, with a powerful motion, he pushed the Pole's arm upwards and thrust the knife into Marek's throat. Isaac held onto the struggling fighter, embedding the broken blade into his Adam's apple as far as the hilt of the knife would allow. He looked into the terrified eyes of Slovoski and in a low, menacing growl, hissed the words.

"Correction ... *You* Lose!"

When Isaac released his hold, Marek fell instantly to his knees, still holding the knife into his own neck as if performing a surreal act of Hara-kiri.

With a last look of despair, Slovoski eventually slumped forward onto the ground ... the fight of the Century, together with his life, now over.

I was speechless, truly speechless. Basically, I had just been told about a murder and I remained wide-eyed and open mouthed for some time. George studied me from over the rim of his mug, no doubt waiting for me to comment. But it was some time coming I can tell you.

"So what happened to Isaac?" I eventually managed. "Was he arrested? Did he go to jail or did he go on the run and hide out somewhere?"

George smiled. "None of the above," he replied calmly. "In fact, the only thing he did do, was give up fighting and return tae fishing full time!"

"What!" I exclaimed. "But surely the Police would have found out that it was Isaac who killed Marek?"

"The Police?" George replied with a chuckle. "The Police already knew son!"

"Eh?" I quizzed bemusedly. "So why wasn't he taken in? ... Murder's a major crime!"

"Aye, it is," George answered casually. "But when there's certain considerations tae be taken intae account ... well!" He raised his mug and took another gulp of his tea, his eyes fixed on mine.

"*Well* what?" I repeated bemusedly. "What sort of considerations? ... you can't just ignore a murder George!"

George wiped his mouth with his hand, looked around and then leant forward as if he was about to reveal some top-secret information. It might have looked more effective had there been more than just the two of us left in the cafe.

"You can when half the local Police Constabulary are already at the venue," he replied in a near whisper. "No' tae mention some well known public figures!"

He gave me a crazy wink, tapped his nose and then leant back into his chair, smiling: no doubt at the stunned look on my face. For the second time in as many minutes, I was shocked.

"So you're telling me that it was covered up? Brushed under the carpet as if it never happened? Come on!"

"Let's just say that it was easier for them tae *clean up* the crime scene than it was tae investigate it," George replied matter of factly. "Especially when they would huv hud tae explain why they were at an *illegal* bare knuckle fight in the first place!"

When I left George later that day (or rather when he decided it was time to go) my head was buzzing from the revelations that the old man had recounted and I found myself unexpectedly and childishly yearning for our next meeting; similar to when I was a young boy I suppose, wishing that the days would speed past so that an impending birthday would come sooner rather than later ... and we all know how frustrating that felt!

I couldn't believe that George had worked for a fisherman-cum-murdering bare-knuckle fighter and found it fantastical that the Police Force, an institution of Law and Order, would be corrupt enough to hide a serious crime rather than be found out that they had attended an illegal sport ... mad!

But in all the excitement and interest of his tale, I had been left with so many unanswered questions. I wanted to know about his wife, the significance of his red tie, why he had stayed on Isaac's trawler for almost three years but, more importantly, what had happened when he came face to face with the ghosts of the Atlantic?

As crazy as it sounds, I honestly couldn't wait until the following week. George was turning out to be quite an interesting man and I eagerly wondered where his *memoirs* might take me next. But, as frustrating as the dictation of life can be, it turned out to be a further four weeks before I actually spoke to George again. And therein lies yet another tale.

###

7

The first week that George didn't show, I was slightly annoyed, especially as I had waited in the rain for near on one and a half hours and got piss wet through for my troubles! *Note to self. Try to remember that if a good old British morning starts out with a bright blue sky, don't assume that the rest of the day will remain the same. Take a goddamn coat!*

The second and third weeks that George didn't show, had my emotions running from wanting to inflict physical harm on the man for wasting my precious time, to worrying that something dire had happened to him. Surprisingly, it was the latter emotion that took more of a hold and by the fourth week, I was even contemplating phoning the local hospitals to see if he had been admitted. It was a strange situation to be in and to be honest, it's a bit difficult to explain seeing as the majority of people have probably never given a tramp a second glance, let alone wanted to write their life story. But imagine if you can, that you go to visit an elderly Uncle or Aunt every week as regular as clockwork and that every week, they are sat there waiting for you, eager to chat your socks off. Now imagine that you have turned up one week and they have seemingly vanished off the face of the Earth. How would you feel? Confused? Worried? Well that's exactly how I felt. And though George wasn't my Uncle, or any other relative for that matter, it was a feeling that was not only uncharacteristic for me but one that was in danger of plaguing my conscience for a long time ... plus, I didn't have any other ideas rolling around my head that I could turn into a novel and that in itself was a real nause!

On the Wednesday of week four following George's disappearance, I went into Piccadilly Gardens as usual, having made the decision that it would be my last attempt to find the Scot before I finally quit and put the whole *Life of a Tramp* concept to bed. And though it would be unfortunate and a little frustrating to draw a line under what could have been an interesting tale, I could only hope that he would at least be okay with whatever it was that had caused his absence. As the time passed by, I began to lose faith that I would ever see him again. I had checked the benches, the bus terminal, the surrounding doorways, the cafe where we had sat and drank copious amounts of tea and still, nothing. Just over an hour after my arrival, I had to admit to myself that there was nothing more I could do and that the time to leave had arrived.

I sighed the sigh of a defeated man and though I gave the gardens one final scan (just for luck you understand?) it seemed that I was left with no other choice than to call it a day and move on. And then, from somewhere just behind me, a gruff, German sounding voice rang out, making me stop in my tracks and smile.

"Haben sie lust auf eine tasse tee?"

I turned around, still smiling and once again came face to face with the man himself, grinning like a Cheshire Cat.

"It's German," George confirmed. "Roughly translated as, *do you fancy a cuppa?*" He stepped towards me and held out his hand, which I took hold of and shook warmly, pleased that the old man was back. "Ah think Ah owe ye an explanation son," he offered genuinely.

"Yes you bloody well do," I said in jest. "But let's get that cup of tea first and then you can fill me in with all the details!"

"Deal," he replied. "Though it'll huv tae be your treat," he added, patting himself down. "Ah seem to have misplaced ma wallet the noo!"

"Now there's a surprise!" I exclaimed sarcastically. "I suppose you wouldn't say no to a bacon butty either, would you?"

George smiled and gave me a little wink. "Dinnae look a gift horse in the mouth son. That's what Ah always say!" he replied with a slight chuckle.

As we strolled off in silence towards our regular eatery, I couldn't help but notice that George had changed slightly in his appearance and not for the worst I must add. It was subtle, but he actually looked cleaner and though he was still wearing the same clothes from when I last saw him, they too seemed a little less grubby. It even looked like he had gotten his usually wild barnet and facial hair trimmed which, in itself, made him look a tad more presentable ... to me anyway. In fact, George's whole persona came across as being quite *chipper*, to coin an old adjective and suddenly, it didn't matter where he had been or what he had been up to. In a testament to my patient nature, I intended to listen to the man's elucidation for his absence, free from judgment, free from malice and, if needed, show the maturity of mind to offer sympathy, understanding and forgiveness in this, the saga of George's return.

"Bloody Prison?" I exclaimed, a bit more loudly than I had intended, causing the seven or eight people in the cafe to look towards our table. "Christ Almighty George!" It didn't take long for my *caring ear* plan to fly right out of the window. George glanced around, smiled awkwardly and then turned back to me with a look of dismay on his weathered face.

"Why don't ye just broadcast it tae everyone son!" he scolded sardonically. "Donae worry about me, eh!"

"Oh, well excuse me!" I retorted and though I had indeed not considered his feelings on hearing this latest scoop, I also thought, *sod it*! To be honest, I wasn't really bothered about George's unfortunate plight at that particular moment, more vexed that this scruffy bloke had been the reason for my wasted visits to City Centre Manchester for the last four weeks whilst he was busy living it up at Her Majesty's pleasure and the taxpayer's expense. "But prison?" I repeated. "Jesus! ... I thought you were dead or ill or something! ... I was actually quite worried for some unknown reason ... How stupid am I?"

George bowed his head as the usual bored looking waitress brought over our order and placed it, unceremoniously, onto the table. To my utter surprise, she gave me a wholly dis-approving glare, shook her head and actually *tutted* before walking away ... Tutted ... like it was my fault! I scowled at her back, willing her to turn around and add something else, mentally daring her to have a go. But in true *arsy teenager working in a dump of a cafe* style, she proved to be very adept at acting like I wasn't even there ... and lucky for her I say.

There then followed an awkward silence as a sheepish looking George busied himself lacing his bacon sandwich with sauce and his tea with sugar and though for a small moment I felt a tiny pang of guilt, I was still keen to learn of the reason for his incarceration.

"So," I started. "What did you go to prison for?"

George stopped stirring his tea and looked directly at me. He had a strange expression on his face that made me think that he was about to tell me to piss off and mind my own business. And to be fair, he would be totally justified in saying it, as it really wasn't my business in the slightest. He looked over his shoulder and then back to me, leaning forward in that peculiar secret agent type manner of his, readying himself to reveal all. I was intrigued and found myself also leaning forward slightly in preparation to receive the word.

"Did ye miss me son?" He asked quietly.

I frowned, suddenly taken aback by such an unexpected question and resorted, embarrassingly, to stammering a reply. "What? ... No! ... I was just ..."

"Ye missed me didn't ye?" he cut in, teasingly.

"You're off your head you," I replied in jest.

"Maybe," George said smiling. "But ye did, didn't ye? Ah can tell!"

And though I merely smiled back at the old man, shaking my head dismissively, I guess he saw from the look on my face that yes, in a strange way, I think I probably did.

8

Four weeks previously, on Saturday 2nd August 2008 to be exact, George had decided that he needed to raise some cash and set about it in the only way a man of his standing in society knew how ... by adopting the *hard done to* face and begging.

Things were going quite well and the general public seemed to be in a very giving mood, filling his polystyrene cup with a favourable amount of loose change. In fact, when he had removed the Euros, three arcade tokens and a black button from his *collection tin*, he found himself to be eleven pounds and thirty-five pence better off. Not bad for a few hours work. Now, like me, I guess that people's first impressions would be that George, a down-and-out, would naturally waiver the use of this money for buying something essential, like food for instance and instead, squander it on alcohol. But, like me, they'd be wrong. George had plans for that cash and he figured that he was over half way towards what he needed to do with it. And no doubt he would have reached his goal if it wasn't for one small obstacle ... The Greater Manchester Police Force, or, to be more precise, *The Beggar Squad*, a team of plain clothed officers with no other objective than to clear the City streets of ... well, Beggars.

They had been watching George for some time, seeing if he would try to solicit funds from any members of the public. It wasn't enough that he merely stood there in silence, holding his cup out, as the squad (and George) knew that, if arrested, the case could be argued that he never actually asked for any money but was given it freely and without coercion. With seemingly no *real crime* in the city to attend to (George's words, not mine) the Officers kept their *target* under surveillance for some time, even walking past him at regular intervals to see if they would be subjected to a request for cash and therefore have their evidence. But George wasn't stupid and had been on the streets for a long time; he knew the score.

"They stick out like a sore thumb," George explained. "And what annoys me, is they think that Ah lack the old grey matter to notice the same faces hoverin' around me every ten or fifteen minutes hopin' that Ah'll slip up!"

"But how can you tell who they are?" I quizzed. "Surely hundreds of people, thousands even, pass by you all the time. You can't keep track of everybody?"

"When you've played this game as long as Ah huv Son," George replied smiling "Ye get tae know the enemy!" He took a napkin from the silver holder on the table and wiped the sauce from the corner of his mouth ... and not before time I might add! "They give themselves away y' see," George continued. "What with their freshly pressed jeans and stupid little earpieces, ye can spot them a mile off!"

"So you evaded arrest then?" I asked.

"No' exactly," George replied, which left me a little confused.

"What do you mean 'not exactly'?" I said, frowning. "Either you got arrested or you didn't!"

"Well ... let's just say that Ah *encouraged* it," he answered in one of his *riddle-me-ree* ways, making me shake my head and hold up my face in my hands. "Ok," he continued. "Ah knew they were hoverin' aboot, right? And it was getting late and Ah thought, what the hell. Ah'll huv a weekend o' free food and drink, warmth and somewhere to shower courtesy of the Polis. Ah'll be oot on Monday ... So Ah waited till one o' the more keen looking flatfoots' walked by and asked him for some spare change and ..."

"You got arrested," I finished. George nodded and I had to smile at the man's unashamed scam. Nice way to get a free *hotel* room for a couple of nights, even if it wasn't exactly the Ritz. But then another thought suddenly crossed my mind. "Hang on," I began with a frown. "You *didn't* get out the following Monday though, did you?"

"Naw, Ah bloody didnae!" George growled through gritted teeth. "The bastards set me up. They ended up charging me with some trumped up '*begging with menace*' offence, whatever that is, and told the Courts that Ah'd 'intimidated' members of the public ... me, intimidating. Ah'm an old fuckin' man for Christ's sake!"

"It's probably 'cause you look like a Wookiee," I said, smiling.

"A what?" George asked with a frown.

"You know? ... A Wookiee? ...Like Chewbacca from Star Wars?" George looked at me with a vacant stare and I knew that the moment was gone. "Never mind George," I sighed. "So what happened in Court then?"

50

"Well, the Magistrate looked at me like Ah had just dropped off his shoe, prattled on about decent folk no' wanting t' be taken advantage of and then sentenced me to twenty one days inside ... pompous bastard!"

"Just for begging? Blimey, that was a bit harsh!"

"And Ah would agree," George answered subduedly. "If it hud been ma first time in front of them, that is!"

And there it was. Turns out that George had been in Court for begging no less than six times in eighteen months, so it was hardly surprising that they were getting just a little bit fed up of seeing him. Still, he did get free food and lodgings and even managed to use the services of a prison barber ... Hell, they even washed his grubby clothes for him whilst he was incarcerated, hence the tidier appearance when I met up with him again.

For George, the risk of going to jail was all part of the life he led, an occupational hazard you could say. He had been inside before, but it was usually only for a night or two following his arrest for being drunk and disorderly and more often than not, at a time that actually suited George down to the ground. But, as he spoke about his recent stay at HMP Strangeways, I sensed that he was angry; not with the system, but with himself, as if the stupidity that had earned him the twenty one day lock up, had also caused him to miss something important. I wondered if it tied in with his mystery appointments that he kept making off to. But as much as I probed, George wasn't for giving anything away ... Not yet at least!

###

9

George soon discovered that working for a man like Isaac Andrews was not without it's perks. The captain's colourful history had not only earned Isaac a great deal of respect from his crew, but also from the locals living ashore, which in turn, brought a certain amount of *gratuities*. For example, he never seemed to pay for a drink at The Jolly Piper, (a public house located close to the docks which was popular amongst fishermen and sailors alike), nor was he ever challenged when he occasionally brought home more fish than his official quota allowed; though George surmised that this was probably due to the fact that the Harbour Master, a man with little scruples, was more than willing to turn a blind eye in return for the odd fresh cod or three. But what began to amaze George was the fact that the longer he worked on Isaac's trawler, the more some of these gratuities would start to come his way. When he had gone into the local bakery one day (a place his mother visited on a regular basis) the Baker studied him as if it were the first time George had ever gone in.

"What'll it be?" he asked with an unusual grin.

"Just a cobbler please," George replied, feeling a little uncomfortable when the Baker winked at him. He watched in bemused silence as the Baker, still smiling, took a loaf off the shelf behind him, wrapped it in paper and then proceeded to pick out a few *fancies* (as his mother called them) from under a glass display case and put them carefully into a box.

"Ye're a hand on Isaac's trawler aren't ye?" he asked whilst tying up the box of cakes with string.

"Aye," George replied cautiously. "What of it?"

The Baker swung quickly round and dropped the bread and cakes onto the counter, making George jump a little. "Then be sure tae give him ma regards and thank him for that lovely Hake he got me!" he said firmly. "Will y'do that son?" George nodded dutifully and held out his money for the bread, feeling a sudden urge to leave quickly. The Baker looked down at George's hand and then back up to his face, smiling. "Put yer money away now laddie," he said quietly, handing him the loaf. "This is ma treat!"

"Oh," said George, a little surprised. "Thanks!"

"And these," the Baker continued, picking up the box of cakes. "Are for yer mother!" George hesitated for a moment, not sure what to do next. "Go on, take them," he encouraged, seeing George's reaction. "Ah know yer mother likes to buy them when she can and ... well ... call it a wee gift!" When George took the box off him, the Baker began to chuckle. "But donae be expecting this type of service awe the time young man!" he said heartily and though George wasn't, it came none the less. And not only from the Baker, but also from the Butcher, the Green Grocer and any other establishment that George entered where the proprietor had reason to know Isaac Andrews.

George didn't think that life could get any better. Until, that was, the night he was sat in The Jolly Piper enjoying a few ales with his captain and crew. And it was Isaac that first spotted the look on George's face.

"Close your mouth George," he said teasingly. "It's no' a pretty sight!" George flinched slightly at the vocal intervention and quickly looked down at the table. Isaac leant in towards him so that the rest of the crew wouldn't hear what he was about to say. "She's quite a looker isn't she?" he said with a grin.

"Who is?" George answered, trying to sound as if he had no idea who his boss meant.

"The girl ye've been gawping over for the last ten minutes!" Isaac replied, nodding towards the bar.

George felt himself redden. "Aye," is all he could manage but felt like he wanted to tell the whole pub that she was the most beautiful thing he had ever seen. Long auburn hair that positively shone, even in the dim ambience of the pub's drab interior. And the brightest green eyes that George had ever seen. He guessed that she was about the same age as he and wondered how, in the last twelve months or so that he had been frequenting The Jolly Piper Public House, he'd not seen her before ... surely he would have remembered this particular vision.

"She's been away in Edinburgh for the last year or so," Isaac offered as if reading George's mind. "Studying tae be a teacher apparently."

"Oh," said George, trying desperately to sound indifferent. "What's ..." He stopped to clear his throat that had suddenly become a little dry. "What's her name?" he finally managed. Isaac shook his head and snorted a laugh. George frowned. "What?" he asked.

Isaac lowered his voice to a near whisper. "That's Lilly," he answered, though seeing George's vacant expression, added. "As in Lilly McBride?" George thought about it for a moment, wondering where he had heard the name before. And then, as the proverbial penny dropped, a pained expression appeared on his face. He glanced quickly at the girl behind the bar and then back to Isaac, dumbfounded. "Aye son," the Captain continued with a wry smirk. "Angus McBride's wee daughter!"

George had never felt so deflated. Angus McBride was the landlord of The Jolly Piper and, from what George had heard, didn't appear to like anybody or anything. He was a stockily built man, six feet in height and with a neck that looked to be similar in circumference to that of George's waist. This was not a man to go upsetting and anyone brave enough to ask his daughter for a date, George surmised, would surely be signing their own death warrant. He decided to steal one more look at Lilly before putting her and the thought of any romantic liaisons firmly to the back of his mind. And besides, why would she show any interest in a fisherman. She could probably have any man she wanted ... Father approving of course. He first checked the position of Angus and only when he was satisfied that the landlord was suitably preoccupied did he allow his eyes to seek out Lilly. What he didn't expect was the fact that Lilly was already staring at him ... and she was smiling. George's stomach flipped over. He returned the smile but looked away quickly not quite knowing where to put himself. *'Take another look George, see if she's still looking at you!'* his own mind urged. *'You know you want to!'* Yes he did and he would, just as soon as he had taken another mouthful of his beer. He tried to make it as casual as he could, but it was no use. He looked straight back towards her not even thinking about where or what her father was doing. And there she was, still staring right back at him, returning the smile. This was like being in Heaven and Hell at the same time. A beautiful girl that was no more than ten feet away (Heaven) but one that he couldn't even speak to for fear of her Father's reaction (Hell). It didn't help that the more ale Isaac consumed, the louder and more frequent his teasing became, causing the odd suspicious look from Angus.

George decided that it was time to leave. He got up from his table and walked to the exit, determined not to glance at Lilly. As he placed his hand on the door handle, an angel sang. "Goodnight George!" Lilly called out.

'How does she know ma name?' George thought. He glanced over his shoulder back towards the bar and there she was again, smiling right at him. "Aye," he replied a little nervously. "Goodnight t' ye too!" He held her in his stare (or was it she that held him) temporarily lost in the tranquillity of her beauty. He could have stood there for hours and probably

55

would have done if it hadn't been for the loud and quite obvious clearing of the throat by the Landlord. George snapped quickly back into reality and left the pub, grateful that the cool night air helped quell the sudden reddening of his cheeks.

I chuckled a little, but couldn't help feel a certain empathy for George, especially as his cheeks had started to take on that crimson glow again as he relived his moment. "I take it you were a bit smitten with this girl then George?"

"Aye son," he replied quietly and honestly. "Ah was indeed. But Ah reckon that any man who ever visited that ale house would have been too, whether they admitted it or not!"

"So did you ever get to speak to her again?" I began and then leant forward, smirking. "Or were you just not really her type old boy?" Yes yes, I know he was reminiscing on a romantic interlude but I couldn't help but add the little wind up.

"No' her type?" George repeated with a forlorn expression on his face and I suddenly felt a pang of remorse for appearing to have hit a particular raw nerve.

"Sorry George, I was only pulling your leg!" I offered.

He stared at me intensely. "Well," he began softly. "Ah don't know if Lilly had a particular *type*, as ye so crudely put it but Ah suppose her beauty and intelligence put her way above ma league anyway!"

I leant back in my chair and bowed my head feeling slightly ashamed.

"After all, what would she see in a fisherman eh?"

'*Alright George, I get the picture*!' I thought.

"No' a lot o'money, nae real prospects! Excuse the pun, but Ah wisnae what ye would call a great catch!"

'*Just how bad is he going to make me feel exactly?*'

"Didnae stop her marrying me though did it?"
"What??" ... I looked up sharply towards his now beaming, weathered face that sported an undeniable *that'll teach you* expression all over it.

"D'ye fancy another cuppa son?" he added, chuckling.

I couldn't help but smile back ... Bastard.

After that night in the pub, George never stopped thinking about Lilly. In fact, ninety nine per cent of his waking hours were spent dedicated to visualising her face, the other one per cent was reserved for secondary, more mundane tasks ... such as eating, breathing and trying to do his job. He found that these activities had become increasingly more difficult to manage; a situation that hadn't gone unnoticed.

"George! ... George, for Christ's sake man!" The booming voice of Isaac brought George sharply back into reality. "Am Ah paying ye to work or daydream awe day? Now haul that fuckin' net and look sharp! There's nae free fuckin' lunches on ma boat son!" Isaac watched the young fisherman jump into action like a startled cat and couldn't help but smile to himself. *'She's got the boy bewitched,'* he thought to himself. *'But what to do about it, that's the question?'*

When he eventually found the courage to enter the pub again, some two weeks later, George quickly scanned the bar area and felt wholly disappointed when he didn't see Lilly standing behind it. Hearing the sound of a female's laughter, his eyes shot towards the entrance of the pub's snug area and stared in hope as the door began to open with a painfully slow momentum. His heart raced as he willed and wished it to be the Landlord's daughter that was making an appearance. But, with a look and a sigh that only served to underline his compounded dismay, George watched on as a locally well-known woman emerged from the snug, hiccupped and then staggered past him towards the exit with a fresh-faced sailor in tow.

"Are ye lookin' for someone George?" Angus asked, causing the crestfallen young man to jolt slightly.

"Who, me?" he replied nervously.

"Well Ah donae see anyone else hingin' aboot ma premises called George, dae you laddie?"

"Well ... Ah ... er," George stammered and looked around the crowded vault, unaware that the question was in fact rhetorical. He was slightly relieved when he spotted Isaac and his crewmates huddled around a table but even more relieved when his boss intercepted the potentially awkward conversation now brewing with Mr McBride.

"Comeoan sit o'er here George before ye cause a scene!" Isaac called. "And can ye fetch him a pint Angus?" he added. "He looks like he needs one!" George bowed his head missing the nod and the wink passed between his Captain and the Landlord.

Angus brought over a fresh round of ales and placed them on the table but rather than walk immediately away, he remained steadfast, staring hard at George. George glanced up and smiled meekly, anxious that the landlord neither smiled back nor broke his gaze. The towering man stayed motionless for a while seemingly studying the young man before him. George felt himself begin to perspire wondering if he had upset Angus in some way and was about to pay dearly. All conversation around the table had stopped as the trawler men's eyes flicked with anticipation between George and Angus.

When the landlord leant down towards him, George recoiled slightly expecting himself to be physically dragged to his feet and become the benefactor of a *smartening up*. What he wasn't expecting were the words ... "Lilly will be back t'morrow. Ye can call on her at six!"

Angus walked away leaving a confused, slightly quaking yet very excited George in his wake. For the second time in as many weeks, Isaac said, "Close your mouth George, it's no' a pretty sight!" George did and replaced it with a rather large smile.

Not for the first time, George gazed out of the cafe window back into his old world and smiled as he relived the moment. It was a smile, I surmised, that would have greeted Lilly all those years ago. It was warm, full of love and somehow respectful ... a smile that is normally reserved for someone special in your life. But morosely, it was his eyes that, yet again, revealed his present feelings and I couldn't help but feel a slight sorrow at the sadness they conveyed. He cleared his throat and sat back in his chair, clearly fighting the glaze that was in danger of overflowing into teardrops. As he took another mouthful of tea, I tactfully looked down at the table and began to fiddle with the serviette holder. Although it felt a little awkward, I remained silent, not wanting to speak or stare at George just in case this compounded his obvious embarrassment. It was a couple of minutes before he eventually spoke again.

"We were married just under a year later," he began quietly. "July sixteenth, nineteen forty eight."

"July sixteenth," I repeated with overt enthusiasm, relieved to be talking again. "That was the date we first sat down together in this cafe!"

"Aye" George confirmed.

"And I remember you saying that it would have been your, hang on ... your sixtieth anniversary, yes?"

"Aye" he repeated. I was now on a little roll.

"And you wore that crazy red tie?" I bundled on regardless.

"Aye ... ma first anniversary present from Lilly!"

Shit! ... "And how nice it was too!" I quickly spluttered with erroneous conviction. Thankfully, George saw the funny side of my failed back peddling attempt.

"It is a wee bit bright isn't it?" he began with a small titter. "But ..." he sighed a little before continuing with obvious sincerity. "It's one of the few things Ah huv left tae remind me of her, 'cept for what's up here!" He began to tap his temple. "And what better time to wear it than on our anniversary?" I nodded in agreement. "Mind you," he said. "It's the only time that Ah *would* wear it!" He looked towards the ceiling before adding. "Sorry Lil!"

I came to the elementary conclusion that Lilly had passed away and though I didn't feel that this subject should be broached, I knew that in time, George would probably tell me anyway.

"So George," I said, moving swiftly on and away from my clanger. "It sounds like you didn't waste much time popping the question then?"

"Why wait?" he replied, shrugging his shoulders. "From the moment Ah saw her, Ah knew that she was the girl Ah wanted to spend the rest o' ma life wi' ... An' luckily for me, she felt the same way!"

"But how come Angus suddenly allowed you to see his daughter?" I quizzed. "I thought he was very protective? ... and a bit of a tyrant?"

"Aye, that he was son," George replied. "And it took him a long time tae warm tae the fact that Ah was courting his Lilly, Ah can tell ye!" He smiled before adding. "But, as Ah discovered on ma wedding day, it turned out that Isaac was actually the man to thank!"

"Isaac?" I asked, frowning. How come?"

"Because," George answered, chuckling. "It appears that even Tyrants can be swayed by a lifetime's supply of free fish!"

10
The Ghosts of The Atlantic (Part One)

When George was relaying the following story to me, I had already decided to remain silently sceptical. Why? Because a casual glance at his large hands, coupled with the stern look on his face, gently convinced me that laughing would not be the wisest of options to choose. Yet, as the tale unfolded, even a cynic like myself couldn't help but feel a slight uneasy chill as George took me back in time to his spectral encounter ... And I certainly didn't expect that!

That said, I will leave you, the open-minded reader, to digest the following account and draw your own conclusion as to its validity ... I am merely a messenger passing on the narration of an old Scot ... But, whatever your end belief may be, I'm sure you will agree, that it's one hell of a tale to be told.

###

At four am on Tuesday 1st February 1949, George woke with a start and hastily turned to face the young woman lying next to him. He sighed with relief that the distress he had felt seconds earlier, had only been the result of a bad dream ... a dream that saw George desperately searching for that same young woman despite everybody in the town (including her father Angus McBride, who had bizarrely taken on the appearance of Isaac Andrews) telling him that, not only was he not married, but that a girl called Lilly, didn't exist.

He propped himself up on his elbow and starred lovingly at his sleeping wife before kissing her gently on the forehead. Lilly smiled and without opening her eyes whispered. "Ah love you George!"

"And Ah you Mrs Bell," he replied, though he doubted she heard as she'd already fallen back into a deep slumber.

He slid out of bed, careful not to wake her for a second time and got quietly dressed. After a bowl of salted porridge and a mug of strong tea, George headed out for work, gasping slightly as he stepped into the cold early morning air. He pulled his worn trench coat tightly around him, thankful that today was the day that clothes rationing would come to an end in Britain and hopefully allow him to purchase some warmer togs. Winter would keep a grip on Scotland for at least a couple of months more. Of that, George had no doubt.

When he reached the harbour gates, George casually glanced up at the large clock above the night watchman's office and was a little shocked to see that he was late ... he could have sworn he had set off early enough. He thought for a moment and quickly came to the conclusion that he could make up for lost time by skirting through the passages running alongside the warehouses and zig zag his way to where The Pearl of Good Hope would be moored. If he walked along the main drag, as was usual, Isaac would probably have set sail way before George had arrived and that would mean only one thing ... unemployment.

George set off at a quick pace, turning down the first walkway that he came to. As the morning sky was still set to the colour of night, George knew that the unlit passages would be quite hazardous, awash with old crates, crumbled masonry and broken glass, not to mention the hoards of rats that scurried around in the dark searching for food. He wondered if a stray human had ever been on their menu and shivered slightly at the thought of being overrun by hundreds of verminous hunters. He forged on with a wary agility, turning this way and that way through the labyrinth of narrow alleys, effortlessly vaulting any discarded crates or mounds of rubble that blocked his path. As he continued, George was confident that he was making good time and would arrive at the trawler with minutes (rather than moments) to spare, ensuring Captain Andrews would be none the wiser. Just this last corner to turn and ...

Halfway into what he believed to be the final passageway that would lead him back to the harbour front, George stopped quickly in his tracks and stared in bemusement at a solid, high wall blocking his egress. '*Ah don't remember that!*' he thought to himself as he began to mentally retrace his steps, wondering where he had gone wrong. As he turned around to face the way he had just come, George frowned at the sudden appearance of a heavy mist swirling all around him, taking his visibility to near zero. "Shite!" he cursed quietly. "That's awe Ah need!" He made his way back along the passageway, slowly, hoping to find the right way out, though he would have put money on his first choice being a certainty.

For what seemed like an eternity, George hurried down alleyway after alleyway as fast as the conditions would allow. But, incredulously, with each new route came yet another dead-end. When he finally stopped, after being confronted by another impassable force, he put his hands on his knees and tried to regain his breath, sweat pouring from his face. "Ah cannae fuckin' believe it!" he said with a frustrated half laugh, half sob. He stood up and looked around, but with the mist now engulfing any possible point of reference, he was beginning to think that he would never find a way out of this maze. He thought about his options and came up with the only fitting solution.

"Hello!" he cried out loudly. "Can anyone hear me?" He was answered only by the sound of silence. '*Surely there must be somebody about?*' he thought before calling out again. "Hello ... Anybody ... Helloooo!" This time, George heard the eerie call of a foghorn from way off in the distance, seemingly taunting him as if this was the only thing that would answer his plea. George sat down on the sodden floor and leant back against a warehouse wall desperately trying to control the small seed of despair that was now beginning to germinate. "Cam doon George," he encouraged himself. "Don't panic man!" But he couldn't help himself. He was lost inside this stupid concrete puzzle and until the fog decided to lift, he would have no way of escaping its hold. He figured that Isaac would have cast off by now anyway but not before cursing his unreliable employee who would probably have to find another job if he had any hope of supporting his wife. And what would Lilly say? She would surely be disappointed. But would they look back and laugh about this bizarre situation in years to come or would she just consider him to be an incapable, useless man not worthy to be with her? Maybe she would leave him and return to her father and then he would be on the wrong side of Angus for failing his daughter and that in itself didn't bear thinking about ... Oh God!

"Are ye lost there laddie?"

To say that George jumped at the unexpected sound of a voice suddenly emulating from the fog, would have been a massive understatement. "Jesus almighty!" he exclaimed, quickly getting to his feet. George fixed a wide eyed stare as a frail and aged looking man appeared to drift out of the mist and reveal himself. "Ye scared me half t'death!"

"But thankfully, no' completely eh?" the old man said with a strange, gravelly cackle. George saw that he was clothed in a fashion that he suspected was at least fifty, if not a hundred years old and it reminded him of the posters he had once seen displayed outside the Glasgow Empire picture house advertising the film, 'The Picture Of Dorian Grey'. His silver, slicked back hair was long enough to sit on his shoulders whilst a gaunt and pale face accentuated his dark sunken eyes ... eyes that George thought, appeared lifeless. He then began to cough with such ferocity that George imagined a lung might actually fly right out of the old man's mouth and land at his feet.

"Are ye alright?" George asked with genuine concern as the stranger showed no signs of recovering. The man raised a dismissive hand whilst continuing to cough into a ragged handkerchief. When he had recovered a little and pulled the piece of cloth away from his mouth, George saw that a thick residue of black, blood infused phlegm had been discharged ... the result, no doubt, of a lifetimes' employment in the Glaswegian copper works. The old man wiped his mouth, put the handkerchief back into his pocket and looked up at George, smiling.

"Fog caught y'out did it son?" he asked brightly.

"Well Ah ..."

"Don't worry," the old man interrupted before George could finish his sentence. "Yer no' the first an' you'll no' be the last Ah expect!"

"But Ah know these passages well!" George exclaimed, feeling a little embarrassed. "Or at least Ah thought Ah did!"

The old man chuckled again, nodding his head. "The fog can do that tae a man ... Lulls ye in tae a false sense of security, an' before y' know it, she's got ye trapped in her lair!" The man grimaced and continued with a tone that was more akin to taking to one's self than anybody else. "An' when that happens, ye best pray that it's a day when she is kind enough to show her benevolence an' let ye be on your way wi' oot paying the Ferryman!" George frowned and wondered what the hell the stranger was going on about. Yet, as the old man raised his head to the heavens, George involuntarily followed suit and looked straight up, the usual canvas of a midnight blue sky blocked by the false ceiling of a murky grey vapour. He remained strangely transfixed as if hypnotised by the fog's silent swirl. "She can be merciless!" the man hissed.

George let out a small startled yelp, hastily snapping his head back to eye level as the man, who had been some ten feet away from him moments earlier, was now inexplicably stood directly at his side. "Bloody hell. How did ye ...?" George started.

"But she likes her wee jokes laddie!" the man interjected again, smiling as he gestured with his head to somewhere beyond George.

Still trying to comprehend the stranger's swift manoeuvre, George frowned before slowly turning to face where he had just motioned. He scanned the mist but could see nothing other than the same solid black wall that had been responsible for putting an end to his plight. "What am Ah suppose tae be lookin' at?" he asked, before turning back around with a puzzled expression. "Ah cannae see anything!"

"Patience laddie, patience," the old man whispered. "But donae just look ... see!" he instructed, sternly.

George sighed and reluctantly turned to face the wall again. He still didn't notice anything different and was beginning to lose his tolerance. "Ah still cannae ..." he began but broke off mid sentence as a small but unnaturally random breeze washed over him, causing something to move by the wall that caught his eye. George squinted and peered hard at the same spot for what felt like an eternity. As nothing seemed to be revealing itself, he decided to give up and concede that he had made a mistake. But suddenly, there it was again and this time there was no mistake ... a small shaft of yellow light radiated through the haze yet mystifyingly, appeared to be coming out of the wall itself. With guarded curiosity, George took a step towards the light but then suddenly stopped to glance back at the stranger, who merely smiled and gave an encouraging nod for him to continue. George moved forward again, careful not to lose his footing on the mounds of debris covering his path. As he got closer, the shaft of light became wider and more prominent, piercing its way through the fog, though George did wonder why it flickered ... not unlike the flame of a candle when exposed to a slight draught he thought.

When he was within a few feet of the light source, George stood on an unstable rise of debris and instinctively put his hand out, hoping to steady himself against the wall. But as soon as his hand made contact, the wall flexed backwards as though it had become suddenly malleable, causing George to lose his balance, stagger like a drunk and finally end up on the seat of his pants. George sat there bewildered whilst behind him, there was a sharp return of the old man's gravelly cackle. "What the fuck!" George exclaimed loudly, before quickly getting back to his feet. He looked at the wall a little more closely, frowned and then carefully touched it again, not quite believing what it was before his eyes. A few moments later, his scowl turned into a feint smile and he shook his head. He listened to the stranger, still beside himself and couldn't help but titter to himself, even if it was at his own expense. Had he bothered to look more closely at the wall in the first place, he would have seen that it had not been constructed using bricks and mortar, but from a large piece of tarpaulin draped over a gas pipe that ran from one warehouse to another. And the mysterious flickering light that he could see was merely the illumination from a harbour lamp on the other side of the 'wall' that shone through intermittently as a loose corner of the tarpaulin sheet flapped gently in the breeze.

A few minutes later George was back on his feet, pulling at the cover in a bid to make a sizeable gap that he could climb through. It wasn't an easy task, as much of it had been tied into place and his hands and arms soon began to ache. As he slowly tried to work his way through the tarpaulin sheet, he was conscious of the fact that the man behind him was still busy laughing away and to be honest, it was beginning to grate on George's nerves ... he was hot and sore and the last thing he needed was an over reacting audience. '*Ah wish he'd shut his mouth!*' George thought as he forged on, when suddenly, to his utter surprise, the laughing stopped. "Thank God for that!" he whispered under his breath.

"It's no' God ye need tae thank George!" the old man shouted just as a large piece of tarpaulin fell to the ground, finally revealing the harbour front.

In a split second, George went from a feeling of exhilaration at suddenly being able to see his way out, to one of total confusion. *'How did he hear that?'* he thought. *'An' how the hell does he know ma name!'* He quickly turned around and stood aghast as his brain tried to make sense of what his eyes could see. As impossible as it seemed, the old man, together with the fog, had now disappeared.

"What? ... As in, vanished into thin air?" I asked with a suspicious look.

"Ah'm no' really sure," George replied, shrugging his shoulders. "One minute he was there, the next ... gone!"

"Well, he probably just went around the corner or something!"

"Maybe," George said. "But how d' ye explain the fog an' the fact that he knew ma name?" he asked abruptly.

"Firstly, he'd probably seen you at the harbour before and knew who you worked for," I began, with my Sherlock Holmes-esque powers of deduction. "And secondly..." I paused, trying to quickly think of a rational explanation for the rapid lifting of the fog whilst all the time being closely watched by a furrow browed old man. "And secondly," I continued. "Maybe a sudden on-shore breeze from the harbour front came in when the tarpaulin fell down and dispersed it!" Ok, even I wasn't convinced by that theory but I wasn't for having any supernatural forces at work here. George just looked at me silently and shook his head.

"And another thing," he said almost matter-of-factly. "When Ah did eventually turn up at the trawler, what dae ya think Isaac said tae me?"

"I don't know ... 'You look like you've seen a ghost George' or 'why you late George?'"

"That's just the thing!" George cried out with mild excitement.

"What is?" I quizzed, confused as ever.

"Ah wisnae late. In fact, Isaac asked me why Ah was so early!"

"I don't get you ... surely your encounter with Vincent Price and the fog from hell made you late?"

George dismissed my quip and continued. "Ye would think so wouldn't ye?" He lowered his voice slightly. "But somehow," he added. "It seemed that time ... well ... it must've stood still!"

He stared at me intensely, no doubt waiting for me to reply with something like. "Oh my God George, you're right ... call Ghostbusters!" But I didn't. Truth is, I could only find it in me to laugh. "Give over man," I said. "Time doesn't stand still, it's impossible!" George however, didn't see the funny side and sat back folding his arms, throwing me a look of utter contempt. "Sorry George," I continued, still chuckling a little. "But there has to be a rational explanation for all of that too. I thought you're ghostly story was pretty good though!"

"Ghostly story?" George repeated with a frown. "Ye think that was it?"

"Well, yes," I answered honestly. "Why, was it not?"

George began to chortle and rubbed his face vigorously before leaning in towards me once more. "That was just the start o' it!"

###

As the trawler chugged it's way out of the harbour towards the greyness of the Atlantic Ocean, George stood at the stern watching the coastline slowly fade from view. He tried desperately to rationalise what had happened to him less than an hour ago, if only for the sake of his own sanity. But the more he thought about it, the more he convinced himself that he had actually witnessed something from the paranormal world. He shivered at the thought.

"Something on yer mind there George?" a voice asked from behind him. For the third time that day, George's heart nearly stopped beating. He jumped round to find Isaac stood directly behind him re-lighting a half smoked cheroot.

"Fuck!" George gasped. "Why is everyone sneakin' up on me t'day?"

Isaac blew out his match, flicked it overboard and studied George. "What d' ye mean?" he asked, frowning. George thought about telling Isaac about his weird experience but quickly decided against it for fear of being laughed off the boat. After all, who wouldn't laugh at such a tale? (*Editorial note: I think George was having a little dig at me here!*)

A few moments of silence passed between the two before George finally answered. "It doesnae matter," he said quietly. "Ah'm just a wee bit tired!" George could see from the look in Isaac's eyes that he wasn't convinced, so quickly walked away before the Captain could press any further.

As the day wore on, George had managed to put the morning's incident somewhere in the back of his mind and was now more concerned with the fact that, after what seemed like hours of sailing, the order to drop the trawler nets had not been given. When he asked one of the crewmembers why, he was told that the Captain had decided to travel much further afield as the stock and variety of fish would be more plentiful and make for a greater catch. George accepted the explanation and continued with his tasks.

Later, whilst George was sat repairing some netting, he felt the trawler slow down considerably, causing him to look sharply up towards the bridge wondering what Isaac was planning. It was at this point that George's mouth fell open. He slowly rose to his feet, unable to believe his eyes, as the Captain's bridge, which stood a mere eight feet or so above the deck, was now completely hidden by a shroud of the thickest fog George had ever seen. What was equally as daunting, is the fact that the fog hadn't drifted in slowly, but had descended on them immediately and without warning. Visions of his experience earlier that morning, flooded back into George's mind and panic took hold. "Captain!" he tried to shout out but the sudden onset of a dry mouth and throat only lent him the ability to whisper. He peered hard into the fog but could neither see nor hear anything other than the soft chug of the boat's engine. In a surreal interlude, he began to imagine that he was completely alone. His breathing became laboured and his heart pounded in his chest, whilst his legs seemed to have lost the power to move, freezing him to the spot. *'Fuck me, fuck me, this is nae good!'* he thought, still feverishly scanning his surroundings in the hope of seeing at least one of his crewmates. He tried to control his erratic panting, taking in the thin, cold air through his nostrils then blowing it out slowly through his mouth. He closed his eyes tightly hoping to quell his anxiety but was immediately and worryingly met by a picture of the old man he'd met on the dockside, grinning psychotically whilst bearing blackened and broken teeth. George whimpered and quickly opened his eyes, as the haunting tones of the old man's voice appeared to seep out of the fog into his own conscience. *'It's no' God ye need to thank George!'*

And then, the engine of the trawler stopped completely, causing the boat to bob like a cork as the waves of an unusually calm sea lapped gently against its sides. George almost collapsed from anxiety yet somehow managed to compose himself and muster up enough vocal strength to shout out. "Isaac!" he called. Nothing. "ISAAC!!" George repeated with more volume, the rising level of angst clearly evident in his trembling tone.

At first, the silence prevailed, broken only by the sound of the ships bell keeping a steady beat to the swaying of the drifting boat. George was almost at his wits end until, at last, he heard a muffled response from his Captain. "It's alright George, just a wee fret o'fog laddie!"

George let out a long, loud sigh whilst tears of relief began to pool in his eyes. He quickly dabbed them away, just in case anybody else saw and began to tease him, as he knew they would. "What's wrong with the engine?" George called out hoping to sound calm, when in fact, he was trying desperately to regain some equanimity.

"Just a wee damp!" Isaac shouted back. "Everyone stay where ye are while Ah fix it. Ah don't want any o' ye fallin' overboard!" And with that, the silence returned, save for the toll of the bell.

George sat down, leant back against the side of the boat and pulled his legs up towards his chest, resting his arms on his knees. Although still a little jittery at not being able to see anybody in the greyish white tomb, the voice of his Captain had given him some reassurance and finally, as the minutes passed, he began to relax. He shook his head and smiled, mildly scolding himself for being a fool and letting his imagination get the better of him. "Daft wee man!" he said to himself, chuckling. Feeling weary, he let his head fall onto his arms and closed his eyes. He heard the clanking of metal against metal as Isaac set about repairing the engine down below and actually drew some solace from the fact that he could now hear something *normal*. But when the hammering stopped, the eerie quiescence quickly returned ... and that was when George first heard it.

The Scot paused as if building up some inner courage to continue the story. I could see from the look on his face that the subject really was rekindling some bad memories and could only hope that he wasn't about to clam up completely. I was literally on the edge of my seat wondering what on Earth it was that he had heard. He rubbed his face again and let out a small groan before staring out of the window. *'Jesus. Don't stop now Georgie Boy!'* I thought as I watched him drift off into his own world. I had to keep him on track and try to stop him from losing the bottle to continue. But what? *'Show some concern,'* I thought. *'That always works!'* I leant forward. "Are you ok George?" I asked with as much solicitude in my voice as I could manage without sounding effeminate.

George turned to me and smiled faintly. "Aye," he replied softly in a tone reserved for Martyrs. "Ah will be!"

"Good man," I said, trying to sound empathetic.

Right then. Concern over. Back to business.

"So what is it you heard then George?" I probed, eager for him to go on. But he looked at me as if silently asking for more encouragement and understanding of his feelings ... basically milking the attention truth be told!

Never the less, I duly obliged and re-engaged the concerned mode. I bought him another cup of tea and a piece of malt loaf and generally blew smoke up his ass for the next ten minutes or so. And then, after my outstanding efforts to get him to *man up*, I ended with the subtle, yet effective line of; "I will understand if you can't carry on George!" ... Predictably, he could.

###

11

The Ghosts of the Atlantic (Part Two)

George looked up quickly and peered into the fog, whilst trying to listen beyond the sound of the waves and the slow melancholic toll of the boat's bell. After a few minutes, he began to wonder if he'd actually heard it at all or if it had just been the product of an over active imagination brought on by earlier events ... Maybe ... But he could have sworn!

Smirking slightly at his own idiocy, George shook his head and was about to dismiss it altogether when suddenly, there it was again, only this time much clearer. The definite sound of somebody sobbing. But what puzzled George is that it wasn't a man's sob (as you might expect on a trawler full of men) but a woman's. Frowning, George rose to his feet and listened hard, trying to pinpoint where the morose tone was actually coming from. As odd as it was, the sound appeared to be coming from somewhere behind him ... which was unlikely, he mused, as the only thing behind him was the sea. Despite this, he found himself glancing over the side of the boat into the gently swirling vapour covering the sea and became inexplicably entranced by its calm. As if hypnotised, George began to lean out over the side of the trawler as though an invisible force was pulling at his very being, urging him to venture into the icy waters. Falling into this particular sea at this particular time of year would almost certainly have brought about George's demise, yet further and further he leant out, regardless of the dangers. And despite a tiny voice from deep within his sub-conscious telling him to stop, he really didn't want to. Why should he? It felt so right!

But then, as if a Guardian Angel had intervened, the sudden thud of a random buoy colliding with the side of the boat, jolted George back to his senses making him horribly aware of the dangerous position his body was now in. He gasped with fearful realisation and immediately shot up straight, holding onto the side rail tightly with both hands to steady himself. "What tha Hell's goin' on?" he rasped, shaking his head, trying to clear it. It was then that he saw something dark move out of the corner of his eye and turned quickly to face it. Nothing. Yet the sobbing continued, growing in clarity and volume. *'That's gettin' closer!'* George thought, feeling the tentacles of fear creeping up through his body and gripping his senses. He wanted to shout out but suddenly felt as though he'd lost the power of speech. He wanted to run but remained frozen as though nailed to the very decking where he now stood. More than anything else, George didn't want to be by himself. *'Where the hell is everybody?'* he thought, looking from left to right. *'Can naebody else hear this?'*

He looked out towards the sea again all too aware that he was now shaking. And then, as if intent on fuelling his dread, the sound of woe stopped, only to be replaced by the haunting cry of a woman's voice radiating from the fog that hung over the sea. "Please Thomas!" it wailed. "Where are you my love?"

George remained spellbound, staring out in solidified terror ... and then he saw it.

The single, drawn figure of a woman, shrouded in what appeared to be a black Victorian dress and shawl, materialised from out of the mist, floating towards the trawler as though suspended by invisible wires. Through his petrified eyes, George saw that the woman was holding something tightly against her chest as though she had no intention of releasing whatever it was for fear of losing it.

"Thomas!" she called again. "I can't find you. Please don't leave me alone!" She feverishly turned her head from left to right as though in a blind search, yet still advanced towards the boat, evidently oblivious to its presence.

George managed to take a small step back as the ghostly vision reached the boat, stopped and hovered only a few feet in front of him, revealing herself completely. He noticed that her lips were void of any colour and how incredibly pale her face was, accentuated by a thick mane of matted black hair. Bizarrely, he imagined that at one time, she had obviously been an undeniably beautiful woman. But here, and now, in the bleak setting of grey, she looked a dishevelled and pained soul, her face contorted with an expression of unprecedented despair that, until now, George had neither experienced nor witnessed ever before. Her sallow skin would have suggested that she was a woman of late years, yet her dark, tearful eyes, that shone as bright as coals against a palette of fresh snow, convinced George that she was in fact, no older than he.

In a rare moment of free will, George managed to steal a glance at the bundle that the woman held so firmly against her bosom and gasped. For in amongst the packaging of an aged and filth ridden pall, lay the motionless body of a baby, its life undoubtedly taken by the malnutrition its dilapidated form now displayed. George looked back at the woman's doleful face and found that his fear was temporarily replaced by a great sorrow. And for the first time in many years, George wept.

Suddenly, as if hearing his quiet lament, the woman gazed directly at George and smiled, a comforting, warm smile that Mothers reserved for the troubled times of their offspring. And then she gazed down towards her child, gently rocking the lifeless infant as she spoke. "Hush now Baby," she whispered. "Daddy will be here soon!"

One of the baby's arms, limp and grey, fell out from beneath the cover revealing a tiny hand. Through glazed eyes, George looked on with rekindled horror as he noticed that two of the fingers were missing ... not merely because they were missing, but because it appeared that they had been violently ripped or chewed off by something, leaving no more than rotting flesh and exposed bone in their place. George gagged and threw a hand up to his mouth as the woman held her child's arm, kissed the fingers and moved it back into the safety of the blanket.

"There now," she said, whilst re-covering the child. "We have to keep Baby warm don't we? And safe from those naughty little rats too!" The woman began to gently stroke the infant's cheek whilst quietly humming a soothing lullaby.

'*Oh my God*,' George thought with accentuated sorrow. '*She disnae even know it's dead!*' And then, with a harsh jolt of realisation, another more wretched thought quickly entered his mind ... a thought that, up until this point, George had uncannily evaded. One that seemed impossible to fathom yet was undeniably factual ... It wasn't just the baby that was dead!

George let out an involuntary, pained gasp that caused the woman to look up quickly and frown.

"Is that you Thomas?" she asked with visible hope.

'*Jesus, she can hear me!*' George considered, adding new confusion and alarm to his already shredded nerves.

The woman began to move forward towards George with a noticeable sense of urgency. "I'm here my darling!" she cried out, heading towards the side of the boat with graceful stealth. George started to edge slowly backwards, thankful that his legs had at last found some movement. He saw the woman float incredulously though the side of the boat as though it didn't exist and hold out her hand expectantly. "Hold me Thomas!" she pleaded. "Please hold me!"

In his panicked retreat, George's feet became entangled in some forgotten netting strewn across the deck causing him to fall backwards, hard and heavy, onto the timbered floor. Despite the sudden surge of pain he felt as his head connected with the wooden boards, he sat up quickly just as the woman came to rest at his feet. "Thomas?" she asked, studying him with a confused grimace.

"No, no!" George screamed. "Ah'm no' Thomas!"

The apparition continued gazing at him for a short while as if trying to decipher his words. Then, with a sudden and loud shriek, her face changed to one of brutal anger, her pale lips pulled back into a snarl revealing broken and blackened teeth. With little warning, she fell towards George.

"NOOO!!" George screamed, holding up his arms to his head in a fruitless attempt to shield himself. In the split second that it took for the woman's aura to pass through him, George felt an incredible, unearthly cold ravage his body, the type of cold that was synonymous with morgues and crypts alike. It consumed his whole being in an instant seemingly trying to infest and condemn his very soul. He smelt a dank, acrid aroma that reminded him of rotting meat and felt his stomach aching to expel its contents as the stench seeped into each and every pore. In a macabre moment, George's mind flashed with images of old ships on rough seas, each full of pitiful men, women and children crying and praying for saviour. But in this particular cinematic display, saviour was not as hand as the ships, battered and ripped apart by the treachery of the violent sea, sank without redemption into a watery grave.

And then, just as soon as it had begun, George's torment stopped. He waited a good while before removing his arms from his head, as if not wanting to believe his nightmare was over. Shaking from the adrenaline rush of fear, he slowly lifted his head and opened his tear-stung eyes, staring at the world around him. The fog had mysteriously lifted, revealing the pale blue of a clear Atlantic sky, whilst crew hands suddenly appeared as the trawler's engines spluttered into life easing her forward once more. George rose unsteadily to his feet and breathed in as much of the cool, salty air as his body would allow, clearing his lungs and his head whilst staring out over the calm waters in quiet, troubled contemplation. Fresh tears began tracking their way down his cheeks as his initial anguish faded once again back into sadness. The tragic plight of those lost souls would remain etched in George's mind for always, like a weeping scar that, even with the passing of time, would not heal.

Not long after that day, George left The Pearl of Good Hope and the fishing industry forever.

I sat in stunned silence, staring intensely at George whilst George stared intensely back at me. All between us was deathly quiet, as we both remained caught up in a moment of fantastical madness. But what sorcery had this man possibly used to bewitch me so and render me speechless? What strange subterfuge had my mind been dealt that I had become lost in a world of old ships, sea storms and a plethora of tragedy? I feared being mentally trapped in another age and time, powerless to return to the present ... But then, as if sensing my angst, the dulcet Scottish tones of George *The Story Teller* Bell, finally broke the hex with an utterance of wisdom inherited from his former Captain.

"Close y' mouth son ... It's no' a pretty sight!"

Neither George nor I ever mentioned his encounter with the supernatural again, though I must admit to having had a thousand and one questions I wanted to put to him at the time.

And it wasn't so much to clarify the points, more to try and disprove his sightings. But something had happened to George since he recounted his story, as if a huge millstone had been taken from around his neck and he could at last close off that part of his life. He seemed more light hearted, more forthcoming and I wasn't about to ruin his new found Karma by continuing my *Doubting Thomas* routine. So I bit my tongue and let it lie, honoured that after all these years, I was apparently the only one he had ever told. As my father once said, "Never challenge privilege Son but accept it in the spirit that it was given!"

To be honest, I never really understood those wonderful words of wisdom, not until this point in my life anyway ... Thanks Dad!

12

For the next twenty years or so, George's life remained relatively uneventful. He had taken up various posts of employment since leaving Isaac's trawler, from a coal delivery man to caretaker of a local church hall and had even done a stint as a general dog's body in his father-in-Law's pub. That particular gig didn't last very long though as Angus (Lilly's Father) took every opportunity to voice bitter disapproval of his daughter's strange choice of husband.

"That's enough Angus," Isaac had once cut in when the landlord's comments appeared to be getting out of hand. "George is a good man and Ah cannae sit here an'..."

"It's awe right Isaac," George interrupted, suddenly appearing from the cellar. All heads turned towards George, including Angus's. "Ye huv more chance o' changing the shape of an arsehole than ye huv o' changing his opinion of me!"

Everybody in the pub roared with laughter, everybody that was, apart from Angus. He scowled at George, lay down a half pulled pint, much to the displeasure of the waiting customer, and turned to face his son-in-law.

"Huv ye a problem George!" he rasped. The laughter in the pub stopped as quickly as it had started, replaced by a sudden wave of tension that caused most of the clientele to bow their heads and pretend to look pre-occupied with their drinks. George stood in awkward silence, shifting his gaze from Angus to the crate of mild he was carrying. "Thought not!" Angus added, turning his attention back to the pint he was pulling. He looked up to the man on the other side of the bar and smiled. "Sorry aboot that Jimmy," he offered. "Thought tha useless little shite wa' tryin' tae punch above his weight there!"

Angus chuckled. The customer didn't and neither did George. There were two things about making that comment that Angus obviously hadn't considered. The first was that, after a few years of hauling fish and heavy labouring, George was no longer *little,* but had developed into a well built young man with the strength to match most men twice his age. And secondly ...

The sound of bottles smashing as the crate fell heavily to the floor made the otherwise serene customers jump out of their skins and turn around just in time to see George advancing quickly towards Angus. The Landlord glanced sideways, frowning at the sudden noise. Unfortunately for Angus, his reaction wasn't quick enough to stop the clenched fist of George connecting with his chin, knocking him backwards. Angus reached out to the shelving next to him in the vain hope of attaining some kind of grip but the momentum of his body had already plotted his final destination. Bottles and glasses crashed onto the floor as Angus's flailing arms ploughed through them during his descent. As he hit the ground, the shock of what had just occurred forced him immediately back to his feet. Not, as you would think, to retaliate, but as an attempt to disguise his embarrassment at being put down by a *boy*. The once hard persona of the landlord now bordered on comical as he quickly scanned the pub looking for anybody who might be laughing at him. Externally, nobody was. But the image of a large red-faced man with a beer soaked shirt and particles of glass in his hair, certainly didn't help the Patrons' self control.

George was heading for the exit when Angus finally refocused and though he had no intention of running after him, he felt that the last word should be his, if only to save face. "Aye, that's right," Angus shouted across the pub. "Run away. An' donae bother comin' back!"

George stopped in his tracks and turned towards Angus, anger still present in his eyes. Thankfully, nobody saw the Landlord gulp. "Do ye see me runnin'?" he asked calmly before addressing the rest of the pub. "Does anybody see me runnin'?" Nobody answered. George looked around at the customers and then back towards Angus. "Y'see Angus?" he continued. "Ah'm no' runnin' anywhere. But ye can take it that Ah've quit!"

A small ripple of mirth sounded around the pub as George turned around to leave. He took hold of the door, glanced sideways and caught sight of Isaac staring back at him. For a short moment, George felt as though he had somehow let his former employer down. He knew that violence wasn't the answer but the provocation over the last few months had proved too much and he hoped that Isaac would at least understand that. George offered a slight smile and felt a surge of instance relief when the Captain not only returned it, but also respectfully nodded and raised his glass. A fitting tribute to a young man who HAD punched above his weight ... and won.

"Bloody hell George!" I gasped. "Way to go. But what did Lilly say about you snotting her old man?"

"Hitting him was no' the issue apparently," he replied, chuckling slightly. "But she wisnae best pleased that Ah'd lost yet another job!"

After a brief moment of laughter, George lowered his eyes slightly, his cheerful expression suddenly turning into a frown as though he was about to impart some dire recollection of his life. I braced myself.

"New top?" he asked, gesturing towards my torso.

"What?" I replied with furrowed brow, more than slightly bewildered as to the sudden and random change of topic. I instinctively looked down at myself, focusing on my brand new, brilliant white, *Diesel* shirt and realised, with horror, exactly what the old man's point was.

"Aw for shit's bleedin' sake!" was my immediate and stentorian comment, an articulation that left the now staring cafe staff and customers with a suspicion that my education and upbringing had probably lain somewhere in between the toilet and the gutter.

"It's only a wee bit o' ketchup," George calmly, but bravely, pointed out. "It'll wash!"

I snatched at a tissue from the overfilled and tightly packed silver dispenser, causing the whole grease ridden, sugar caked, useless thing to fly across the table, bounce against my chest and land on my lap, adding a further stain to my shirt in the process.

"Jesus Christ!" I screeched in disbelief, holding up my arms. "Why don't I just pour the whole shitty table all over me and have done with it!"

Whilst I hastily pulled tissues out of the holder, head bowed and seething, I suddenly heard a strange, muffled whimpering sound, a bit like the sound a new puppy makes when quietly yearning for its mother. I quickly looked up wondering who the hell had brought a bloody animal into a cafe, poised to give them a piece of my mind which given my current state, wouldn't have been a nice piece I can tell you.

As if to add to my torment and push my annoyance to another level, I immediately discovered the source of the peculiar noise. It wasn't a dog as first suspected ... oh no, dear reader ... it wasn't even close to being an animal. What it was, was the old sod sat opposite me, head down, shoulders bouncing up and down as though an invisible puppet master, controlling his movements, had developed a bad case of the shakes. His hand was held up to his face as his fingers squeezed his nostrils together in a futile attempt to quell the laughter. The result ... an unusual whistling, squeaky, high-pitched girly whimper ... just like a stupid dog ... bastard!

"Oh yeah," I began sarcastically. "Bleedin' hilarious that George! Don't worry that my fifty quid shirt is ruined 'cause the lazy sods in here can't be arsed wiping the tables!" The latter half of my comment purposely rose in volume as I cast an evil eye towards the bored waitress. She stared back at me with that unmistakable *give a shit* expression before quickly turning her attention back towards a now smoking and charred teacake sat under the grill ... '*Ha!*' I thought with great delight and maturity. '*That'll teach you to smirk!*'

I returned my glare towards George just as he began to look up, his face red, his eyes streaming with tears. "Sorry son," he offered. "But it was the tissue holder ... Ah couldnae help it!" And off he went again, laughing at me.

I sighed heavily and shook my head before turning my attention back to my shirt, dabbing at the sticky red blob with a spit moistened tissue. This pointless action served only two purposes. The first, whilst initially removing much of the crimson goo from the surface of my shirt, left me with an equally annoying pink smear embedded in the fabric. And the

---

84

second? ... Well, the second was that it encouraged Georgie boy to poke his nose in and proffer his unrequested advice.

"Ye need to get some bicarbonate o' soda on that," he suggested.

"Thanks for that George," I replied sharply, stopping to look up at him. "But can you possibly believe it?" I added with an exaggerated snort and a feigned look of disappointment. "I seem to have left that little gem of the cleaning world right at home today ... how stupid of me!" Well, I wasn't really in the best of moods for receiving laundry advice off a Tramp just at that moment!

Now, having spoken to George for some weeks, I assumed that there was little left he could do which would actually surprise me. I was wrong. He reached into one of his pockets and produced a small, clear plastic bag containing a white powdery substance. "Ye can borrow some of mine if ye like?" he said casually and threw the plastic bag across the table to me. I looked at the bag with disbelief, back towards a smiling George and then back to the bag again.

"You actually carry bicarbonate of soda around with you?" I asked incredulously.

"Ne'er wi' oot it son," he replied, as if to possess it was a requirement by law. "Now wet your finger, dab it into the soda and gently rub it on the stain!" I shrugged, opened the bag and hypnotically followed the Scot's instructions ... after all, what had I got to lose?

"Aye, that's it ... no' tae hard though!" He continued, as if presenting a segment from *Blue Peter*. "Now put a wee bit more on it," he encouraged. In my haste, I re-moistened the same finger and immediately tasted a sharp salty fizz. I pulled a face and grunted my disapproval. "Donae be so soft," George laughed. "Dip it in and ... aye, that's right ... now rub it ...gently now! His slightly excited, broken monologue was starting to sound more akin to a pornographic movie than a

85

cleaning tip, so I quickly intervened to reduce the risk of somebody overhearing and drawing the wrong conclusions.

"Ok George, I've got the idea thanks!" I said, continuing with the cleaning process. After several more dips into the bicarbonate of soda, followed by careful application to the shirt, I was relieved to see that the stain had all but disappeared. I had even gotten used to the unpleasant taste. A final wipe with a tissue and it was as good as new ... well, almost.

"Y'see," George began. "Told ya it would work!"

I looked up at his smug face and eventually managed a faint smile of gratitude. Then something suddenly occurred to me. Something that I hadn't noticed before but now struck me as being a little odd. Why would George, who was dressed in all dark attire, have a substance that, for all intents and purposes, was used to remove stains from white clothing? The subject needed to be broached so I asked the question.

"Ah mostly use it to clean ma teeth!" George replied, purposely producing a sickly wide grin.

I frowned and felt slightly nauseous, as I looked down at the packet on the table and then at my finger, recalling that I had actually tasted his *toothpaste*. But I needed to cover my mouth against the onset of a dry wretch when he casually added. "And of course, ma briefs need occasional maintenance too!"

13

During the latter half of the 1960s, George experienced his longest period of unemployment yet, running from the summer of 1966 to the winter of 1969. Though his wife Lilly was bringing in a wage from her position as a teacher, it was barely enough to cover the basic utility bills let alone put food on the table and so the struggle to make ends meet grew steadily worse. In a testament to his stubbornness, Lilly's father refused to offer any help, maintaining the belief that his daughter would soon tire of George's inability to provide for her and leave him in favour of returning *home*. But Angus underestimated the power of two very important factors; the inherent stubbornness of Lilly and the couple's undeniable love for each other which, even in the difficult times, never waned.

Isaac Andrews looked on their situation with quiet concern and though he had often supplied the couple with fresh fish and the occasional monetary *sub*, he didn't want to be seen as interfering or taking sides for fear of it encouraging some awkward questions. The community that they lived in was large enough to be called a town, but small enough for everyone to know everybody else's business and Isaac wanted to be sure that a particular part of his *private* life remained just that ... for the time being at least.

In the November of 1969, George eventually found temporary employment as a stacker in a warehouse by the docks. The hours were long, the work was physically demanding and the pay was minimal but it gave him a new found sense of being. More importantly for George, he would at last be able to start repaying the man who had selflessly helped him out so many times in the past.

On the day that George received his first pay packet, he walked directly into the Jolly Piper pub for the first time since the whole *Angus-gate* episode. He ignored the glare of surprised disgust from the landlord, (who looked like he was about to protest but thought better of it) and went straight to the man who he knew would be sat in his usual place. As he approached Isaac, his smile quickly faded when he noticed that his former boss looked quite unwell. "Are ye ok?" he asked, more out of concern than a casual salutation.

"Aye son," he replied. "Why shouldn't Ah be?"

"Nae reason," George lied, suddenly feeling compelled to be a little conservative with the truth. "Ye jus' look a wee tired, that's all!" What he really wanted to say was, '*Ye look like shite man!*'

"Nothing a few more of these wullnae put right," Isaac said, raising up his half empty glass with a slight smile.

George wasn't convinced but knew not to labour the point, as Isaac, being a proud man, wouldn't have told him if there was anything wrong anyway.

"So," Isaac continued, staring at George "Ah take it ye're no' here for a dram?"

George immediately re-fixed a smile on his face, mildly excited that he could now reveal the purpose of his visit. "Well," he chirped, reaching into his pocket. He produced a bundle of ten-shilling notes and held them out towards Isaac. The Captain looked at the money, frowned and then looked back towards George. "It's part o' what Ah owe you!" George explained, pleased that he was able to offer at least something towards his debt.

Isaac held George in his stare for a while before gesturing towards a chair. "Sit down George," he quietly instructed. George's smile wavered a little and though he obeyed the direction, felt a little confused as to why Isaac hadn't taken the money off him. Isaac smiled as he looked intensely at George. "How's Lilly?" he asked, taking George by surprise.

"Lilly? ... Aye, she's fine ... But why are ...?"

"An' does it no' bother ye that she hasnae given ye a bairn yet?" Isaac continued before George could finish. "After all, you've been married what? ... twenty years?"

George bowed his head feeling his face redden, not just from embarrassment but also from a sudden surge of defensive anger. After all, what right had this man got to be prying into such personal affairs? It was none of his business that the Bells' hadn't yet produced any offspring ... nor anybody else's business for that matter. But for the moment, George bit his lip, deciding to let the comment pass over his head.

"Ah'm surprised yer still with her," Isaac added before taking a mouthful of his ale. This time, George did react.

"Wha' tha hell do ye mean by that?" he spat, quickly looking up towards Isaac.

"Well," Isaac continued, leaning back in his chair. "Do ye no' sometimes think that ye might be better off with a lassie who is more ... how shall Ah put it? ... fertile!" George couldn't believe his ears. "After all, huving bairns is important for carrying on your family name and if Lilly cannae huv ..." George suddenly jumped up out of his seat, cutting Isaac off mid-sentence. He had heard enough from the old man and his unusually cutting remarks and despite their history, wasn't having him speak about his wife with such disrespect.

"That's enough!" George snapped loudly, causing Angus to look up from the behind the bar.

"Everything awe right there Isaac?" he asked, hoping that it wasn't so that he could expel George from his pub. He couldn't disguise his disappointment when Isaac smiled and waved a dismissive hand indicating that all was fine. "Aye well," Angus added, scowling at George. "Jus' tell your *guest* to keep it down. Ma customers like their peace!"

George studied the only other three people sat around the pub, each staring into their beer glasses and lost in their own private worlds, oblivious to the fact that he was even there. He shook his head and turned back to Isaac, trying to control the urge to bawl at the Captain. "Whatever thoughts ye huv in that sea salted heed of yours Isaac," George continued firmly, though a little more quietly. "Ah suggest ye keep them tae yourself!" Isaac remained silent, guessing that George hadn't finished. He guessed correctly. "Ah married Lilly because Ah love her, no' because Ah wanted bairns. And no' matter wha' ye or anyone else thinks, Ah donae care if she has none or a hundred bairns 'cause the only thing that's important to me is her, no' the continuance of ma bloody family name ... she's awe the family Ah need! But wha' would ye know aboot that, ye donae even huv a bloody family!"

This time it was Isaac that bowed his head, filling George with immediate regret. The old man had, in so many ways, been like a father to him over the years and to Isaac, George had been like the son he'd never had. To Isaac, George was his family.

George wished that he could have taken those words back. He wanted to apologise, to say something that would retract the last part of his speech and let Isaac know that it was just a *heat of the moment* reaction. But the silence remained, becoming more and more uncomfortable as the seconds passed. George looked at the banknotes he still had in his hand, now crumpled and damp from the sweat of his palm, and laid them on the table next to Isaac's glass. "Ah will pay ye back the rest as soon as Ah can!" he said quietly before turning to walk away.

Isaac looked briefly at the money and then up towards George now moving slowly towards the exit. He contemplated his next move, quickly weighing up the pros and cons of the choice he now needed to make. Should he let George leave and be none the wiser or should he call him back and explain everything? As the pub door closed behind George, Isaac had made his decision.

###

George stepped out of The Jolly Piper pub into a bright yet cold winter's afternoon, shielding his eyes whilst they adjusted to the sudden and dramatic change of light. His mind raced as he tried to comprehend what had just occurred between him and Isaac and why the man had felt the need to be so cuttingly direct. He knew that Isaac was a man who often spoke his mind and had witnessed his rants on several occasions in the past, but it was never so personal.

George sighed and shook his head, resigning himself to the fact that no explanation could be fathomed whilst standing outside the pub and decided to walk towards the harbour's edge. He hoped that the stroll would help clear his head, although he suspected that it would take a lot more than a fresh sea breeze to quell the sadness he now felt.

As he walked, George remained oblivious to the many moored fishing vessels he passed until he suddenly found himself stood next to The Pearl of Good Hope gently bobbing on the calm lap of the sea. He looked down at the old boat that had long since been decommissioned as a working trawler and smiled fondly. Sitting down on the cold, stone harbour wall, he turned his face up towards the sky, closed his eyes and allowed the struggling warmth of the sun to wash over him as old memories displaced his current thoughts. George had no idea how long he had been sat there when he was unexpectedly jarred from his meditation, but he jumped just the same.

"Do ye mind if Ah join ye George?" the familiar voice asked. George looked up at Isaac, squinting slightly as his eyes re-adjusted to the brightness of the day.

"It's a free country," George replied, with a tone that was far removed from inviting and looked back out towards the sea. With what seemed like a pained effort, Isaac sat directly next to George and let out a grunt, that caused George to look back at him and frown. "Ye awe right?" he asked, unable to mask his concern.

"Aye," Isaac replied. "But ma limbs are no' as young as they use tae be!" He smiled at George but his former employee merely looked away again, not wanting to make eye contact with a man who had earlier spoken out with such bitterness. After a few minutes of uneasy reticence, Isaac let out a long sigh and smiled again, gesturing towards his boat as he spoke. "She's still the best fishing boat in this harbour," he said chirpily, hoping to engage George in a conversation. George turned sharply towards Isaac, scowling.

"What is it ye want Isaac?" he hissed. "Huv ye come tae apologise for the way ye spoke t' me in the pub? ... If no', Ah would like ye tae leave!" He held Isaac firmly in his stare, waiting for the man to answer. But George's expression quickly softened when he saw an unusual look in Isaac's eyes. Was that sorrow he could see? Well yes, a trace of sorrow was certainly present, but there was something more ... something that George had never witnessed in this man nor, he suspected, had anybody else ... it was a look of fear ... Isaac was actually afraid of something.

"There's something Ah need to tell ye George," he began quietly. "If ye will allow me?" George nodded slightly but said nothing, curious to hear what the old man had to say for himself.

Just under an hour later, George watched Isaac walk slowly back along the harbour wall until he was no longer in view. His mind raced from the incredible story that Isaac had just imparted and wondered why, after all these years, he had only just decided to share such a revelation. It would be an hour later before a stunned George headed for home.

Less than a fortnight after speaking with George, Isaac was mentioned within a small column of the Evening Post:

"ANDREWS, ISAAC: Born 2nd January 1904. Passed away peacefully at his home on 5th December 1969 aged 65 years ... A friend of many who will be sadly missed ... May he rest in peace!"

I felt an unusual sadness for the passing of a man I would never have known existed if it hadn't been for meeting George. But after listening to all the fond narration by the Scot over the past few months, it was clear that Isaac had played a huge part in George's life and it was impossible not to feel some sorrow. I wondered if this traumatic event was in any way connected to George eventually becoming a vagrant, like a small seed of destiny had been sown that would determine his life's path? Deep I know, but suddenly finding out who your real father is, only to lose him to the Grim Reaper less than a week later, must have had an almighty effect on George's Karma. I gave him the customary minute or two before I began my usual subtle and compassionate interrogation.

"Bet that news messed with your head?" I started, with the best empathetic look I could muster. "Especially when your new found dad passed away so quickly afterwards!"

George frowned a little, shook his head and then chuckled softly to himself.

"What?" I quizzed, slightly confused with the man's reaction. "He was your dad, wasn't he?"

Thankfully, George thrived on setting me straight and with a little clarification, it soon became apparent that my understanding of the story had been a tad mis-placed. Isaac had been a father ... but not to George!

14

Two weeks after the passing of Isaac, George received a letter requesting that he and his wife attend the offices of

McKewan & Patterson Solicitors at their earliest convenience, regarding a '*matter of some importance!*'

"Ah huvnae got a suit!" were George's first words once Lilly had finished reading the letter.

"Ye're no' up before the Magistrate George," Lilly teased. "It's probably jus' a reading of his Will Ah suppose. A shirt and tie will be just fine."

"Well Ah huvnae even got a tie," George remarked but then saw the look on his wife's face and quickly checked himself. "Apart from the lovely red one ye bought me of course ... but Ah've no shirt tae match!"

Three days before Christmas 1969, George and Lilly were sat in two high backed, red leather chairs in an antiquated, oak panelled office of Messrs McKewan & Patterson. One of the office walls was donned with several oil paintings of rather important looking gentlemen that George imagined must have been past partners of the company, as he didn't recognise any of them. However, taking pride of place above an intricately hand crafted Adams fireplace, was a duplicated painting of a Lady that he had no problem recognising and quietly wondered just how many establishments throughout Great Britain housed the exact same image of Queen Elizabeth II.

Opposite them, behind one of the largest and most highly polished desks George had ever seen, sat a burly, red-faced, man in a dark, well tailored suit that Lilly thought likened him to Orson Wells ... George would later dispute this with Lilly, stating that the man just looked like an overpaid, pompous ass with glasses; although he would then admit that the comment was just borne out of his own dis-comfort at being sat there wearing a check shirt with an un-matching bright red tie.

In the corner of the room stood an ornate Grandmother clock, the methodical tick of its swaying pendulum breaking an otherwise silent ambience that George was finding somewhat unbearable. He shuffled in his seat like a child who wouldn't settle, earning him a stern look of reproach from Lilly. When the clock let out a single chime, signalling half an hour past ten o'clock, Harold Patterson looked up from the papers on his desk towards George and Lilly and smiled; a smile, George surmised, that was reserved exclusively for these sorts of occasions.

Patterson cleared his throat before speaking and though George expected a loud and brash tone from a man of such stature, was surprised to hear a calmingly mellow, almost hypnotic voice emerge from the solicitor's mouth.

"Well," he began, looking directly at the lady sitting opposite him. "May I start by saying what a privilege it was to have known Mr Andrews and would like to express my deepest condolences to you for your sad loss!"

Lilly nodded slightly in acknowledgment of his sentiments but wondered why he hadn't directed his practised sorrow speech towards George as well ... after all, they had both known him.

"Now," Patterson continued. "As McKewan and Patterson are the nominated Trustees of Mr Andrews estate, I can attest that the Will is quite in order and that he has been extremely thorough and specific with his instructions. As such, his directions are quite straightforward." The solicitor smiled at the couple. "And so, without further ado," he added, looking back down to the papers sat on his desk whilst clearing his throat once again. "This is the last Will and Testament of Isaac Andrews..." he began to read aloud. As the opening script and documented legalities of the Will were read out, George's mind wandered back to his last conversation with Isaac. He would never have imagined at the time, that only three weeks later he would be sat in this office listening to the man's last wishes being read out and he felt a sadness wash over him. The only consolation in this tragic situation was that he and Isaac had parted on good terms that day by the harbour, leaving George with a renewed fondness for his former Captain. But he had also had an insight of the man's troubled mind, an insight that had shocked George and left him with the burden of what to do with the information that Isaac had imparted. In retrospect, it was as if Isaac had known that his days were numbered and wanted to be at peace with himself before passing away. Though George believed that he had somehow helped with that transition, he couldn't decide if he felt honoured to have been a confidant or cursed. What he did know was that he missed Isaac and regretted not telling him how much he really cared ... a sentiment that so many people develop when somebody close to them passes away.

"To George Alexander Bell ..."

Surprised at hearing his name being mentioned, George snapped out of his temporary daydream and shifted awkwardly in his chair as he focused on Mr Patterson.

"... whom I consider, not only to be a good friend but a man I would have been proud to call my Son ..."

George bowed his head.

"... I give and bequeath in its entirety ... including all the rights and entitlements connected with same as established within the Maritime Register ... my fishing vessel, The Pearl of Good Hope, to do with as he wishes ..."

George looked up open-mouthed towards Patterson, shocked at his unexpected *inheritance*. "He left it to me? Are ye sure Mr Patterson?"

The solicitor looked up from the desk and smiled meekly at George. "Quite sure Mr Bell," he said, a little piqued that his flow had been interrupted. "As I pointed out earlier, Mr Andrews has been quite specific with his instructions!" He paused a moment before adding. "And he has also bequeathed the sum of ..." He glanced down at the Will. "One thousand guineas to be used in favour of any future maintenance that the vessel might require!" George gasped. "Though I must point out Mr Bell," Patterson continued, looking back at George. "That should you wish to put The Pearl of Good Hope up for sale on the open market within one year of taking ownership, then that sum, together with any monies accrued as a result of the sale, must be repaid by yourself into Mr Andrew's estate and be reallocated amongst the remaining beneficiaries ... do you understand Mr Bell?" George nodded before Patterson lowered his eyes towards his desk once more. "Now, where was I?"

In the short period of silence that followed, George turned towards his wife. "He left The Pearl to me," he whispered, as though she had somehow missed the news.

Lilly smiled. "Aye love, Ah heard!" she replied softly.

"Aye, o'course y'did ... sorry ... but Ah hud nae idea that ... !" His voice trailed off as a lump entered his throat. When his eyes began to glaze slightly, Lilly reached over and took a hold of his hand.

"He thought a lot of you George," she quietly pointed out. "But ye must be the only one who it wisnae obvious to!" She smiled and gently squeezed George's hand as a single tear rolled down his cheek. Lilly turned back towards the solicitor who had watched the emotional interlude and waited patiently for his cue to continue. "Please, carry on Mr Patterson!" Lilly encouraged softly.

Patterson nodded his head in silent acknowledgement of the instruction, cleared his throat for a third time and fixed his eyes back onto the documents. '*If the news of inheriting an aged fishing trawler has caused such an emotional stir,*' Patterson mused, '*then imagine what the next revelations will produce!*'

###

15

George hovered awkwardly by the kitchen door, staring silently at his wife. Lilly was sitting in an armchair, staring silently into the fireplace, the pages of a letter she had been given earlier by Mr Patterson, resting on her lap. It had been almost an hour since they had returned from the solicitor's office and Lilly hadn't uttered a single word. What's more, she hadn't even bothered to remove her coat and this in itself worried George, as he knew that she was a stickler for outdoor clothing being worn exclusively outdoors ... '*Only dog's wear their coats inside the house!*' she had once pointed out to George when he had entered the lounge donning his trench coat. And George was all too aware that she was only half-joking with him ... he never did it again.

The truth was, George had never seen Lilly like this before and hadn't the faintest idea what to do next. If the roles had been reversed, he knew that she would have asked all the right questions, had all the right answers and afforded all the time in the world to make things better. That's what he loved about her: her uncanny ability to rationalise and quantify any situation, good or bad.

But the roles weren't reversed and not being Lilly, George found himself at a loss as to how he could fix this situation; a situation, he thought, that might have been made a little easier had he bothered to say something earlier. But he hadn't. Instead, he had kept his counsel and stupidly believed (or hoped) that the solicitor wouldn't have mentioned the finer details of Isaac's Will ... Stupid!

He opened his mouth to speak but realised that he didn't have anything constructive to say so quickly closed it. Not since his first date with Lilly had he ever felt so nervous of speaking to her and conceded that he only had himself to blame. With a sigh, he walked into the kitchen and sat at the kitchen table, resting his head in his hands as he reflected on that morning's events.

"And so," Patterson had continued, after naming a couple more beneficiaries and further stipulations within Isaac's Will. "I find myself at the main, and no doubt the more pertinent residue of Mr Andrew's estate, which encompasses both his property at Green Bank and indeed, an amount of cash, all of which has been left to ..."

"Ah never knew he owned Green Bank," declared George, turning to his wife.

"Aye," Lilly responded. "He's owned it for years!" She smiled warmly at the look of utter surprise on her husband's face before adding, "Why, who did ye think owned it?"

"Well, Ah ..." George began, but was cut short by yet another, more pronounced clearing of the throat by the solicitor, making it plain that he was keen to move on. "That's a nasty wee cough ye have developing there Mr Patterson," George said, giving the solicitor a noticeable look of contempt at his abruptness.

Patterson, reddening slightly at the glare he had just received from the well-built man opposite him, quickly lowered his head and located the point of the Will where he had left off. "Yes, ahem ... well, as I was saying," He removed his spectacles and gave them a small rub with his handkerchief hoping to buy a little time to regain some composure before he continued. "The property, as mentioned, together with a cash

sum in the amount of ..." He turned over the page of the Will.
"Ten thousand guineas ..."

"What?" Both George and Lilly cried in unison.

"Ten thousand Guineas," repeated Mr Patterson, though
determined not to be interrupted once again by the inevitable
whys and wherefores that another pause in proceedings would
allow, forged on relentlessly. "Is hereby bequeathed in its
entirety to my sole heir and daughter ..." One of the Bell's
frowned, the other gulped. "Mrs Lillian Bell (nee McBride) to
do with as she wishes!"

Had a pin have dropped in the solicitor's office at that
moment in time, the resultant sound would have been
deafening.

"Bloody Hell!" I exclaimed in astonishment. "So Isaac
was Lilly's dad, not yours?"

George grunted.

"And that is what he told you, that day by the harbour?"

Another grunt followed.

"And did he tell you about his Will?"

George shook his head. "Ah didnae even think he hud
anything worth putting in a Will, so finding out what he
actually did huv was quite a shock ... more so for Lilly,
obviously!"

I pondered for a while before asking the sixty four
thousand dollar question. "So how come you didn't tell Lilly
that Isaac was her real dad?"

George let out a sigh that made him sound weary and I
wondered if I was prying into a part of his life that perhaps was
not for the telling. Nevertheless, after a few moments of
silence, George began to explain. "That day, at the harbour,
Isaac apologised for the way he hud spoken to me in the pub.
He said he wanted tae challenge me, tae see how strong my

love for Lilly was and tae satisfy himself that she would be cherished and cared for no matter what life threw at her. Ah told him firmly that there wisnae any worries on that score, but asked him why he was so concerned ... it wisnae like they were related or anything!"

"At which point he told you they were?" I interjected softly.

"Aye," George replied. "Apparently, he'd hud an affair with Lilly's mum and she ended up falling pregnant. Isaac was over the moon and even suggested that they run away and start a new life together ... all three of them!"

"So why didn't they?" I asked.

George shrugged. "He loved that woman with all his heart," he replied tenderly. "But the truth was, he knew she didnae love him back in the same way and besides, she hud always said that she'd no' leave Angus!"

"Harsh," I pronounced. "But she couldn't have loved Angus either, not if she was having an affair!"

"Aye, maybe," George replied. "But sometimes ye huv to look at the bigger picture and Ah suppose that's what she did!" I frowned as he paused to slurp his tea, not quite following his reasoning. George saw this, wiped his mouth and continued. "Y'see, in those days, it was more about not bringing shame on your family than it was about love and hud she huv run away, then Angus would've had to bear that shame despite the fact that he'd huv been the innocent party!"

"That seems a little unfair," I said. "Especially as she was the one playing away!"

"Oh, her name would huv been mud alright. But then the gossipmongers would've started to question why Angus, a husband and respected member of the community, wasn't man enough to keep his own wife in check. He'd huv become a laughing stock and Margaret, Lilly's mum, widnae huv wanted that ... plus, staying with Angus meant more security for her an' the bairn, even if it did mean hiding the truth and letting him think that he was the father!"

"What? And Isaac just let that happen?"

"He hudnae choice son. Oh, he could've told everyone aye, but what would that huv achieved? ... At least this way, he could watch his child grow up knowing that she would be cared for!"

"That must have been hard, watching his own daughter being brought up by another man and not being able to say anything! ... Quite ironic really, given that Isaac was never afraid to speak his mind!"

"What was ironic," George chuckled. "Is that Angus asked him to be Godfather at Lilly's christening!"

We both smiled for a moment at Isaac's unfortunate predicament before George let out another weary sigh and stared out of the window, back into another time.

"You ok?" I asked genuinely.

He looked back at me with a noticeable glaze in his eyes and when he spoke, his voice had become tainted with an obvious remorse. "Ah never kept anything from Lilly in all the time she was alive," he began quietly. "But Isaac made me swear ... " His voice trailed off as he dropped his head and began clenching his fists; not in anger at anybody else but in a display of annoyance towards himself. "Ah should huv told her," he continued still looking down. "Maybe it widnae huv been such a bloody shock!" He looked back up towards me with an unusual expression on his face: as though pride, sorrow and angst were fighting for the only available spot. "But Ah was true tae ma word ..." he went on. "Even when we heard about the Will, Ah kept my big mouth shut!" He jabbed his finger towards his lips several times as if verifying what he meant by his mouth and then quickly tapped the same finger against his temple. " Ah didnae think for one minute that Isaac would mention it in the bloody thing ... how stupid was Ah?"

"You weren't stupid George," I replied. "You were doing what you thought was right, being a good friend whilst protecting the feelings of your wife. There's no point in beating yourself up over it. Anyone would have done the same!"

George thought about this for a while and then shrugged. "Maybe!" he offered quietly.

As if from a scene of the old, yet magical children's television programme *Mr Benn*, the waitress suddenly appeared by my side bearing two fresh mugs of tea. I looked up at her, forced a smile and offered my thanks. I nearly fell off my chair when the normally *Little Miss Can't-Be-Bothered* actually returned the smile and muttered what sounded like, "You're welcome!"

"What's got intae her?" George whispered as he watched her walk away.

"Decoy tactics," I replied succinctly. George looked at me, confused. "Well," I continued bitterly. "She obviously wanted to avert my eyes away from seeing the state of this crappy mug!" George looked down at my cup and chortled. I snatched a tissue from the holder and attempted (in vain) to remove the heavily ingrained red lipstick marks from the rim of my crockery whilst mumbling a few obscenities.

Whilst I was wondering if the cafe owners had ever heard of that popular concept called *washing up liquid*, I noticed George reaching in and out of his many pockets as though searching for a particular item. "Ah want tae show ye something," he said, catching my stare. "Ah jus' need tae find it first!"

Now, if I'm being honest, I have to tell you that I panicked slightly at this point. Why? Because at the moment in time, haunting memories of the bicarbonate of soda incident came flooding back into my mind and I could only imagine with horror, what aged and used cleaning product he was about to unleash on me next. You see, the thought of him producing some *lipstick removal aid* only to inform me, mid-use, that he'd also found it particularly effective for de-lousing the crack of his arse, was an image that I didn't really want floating around my sub conscience for eternity ... bizarre and totally irrational I know but it didn't stop me from putting my head down and start vigorously rubbing my cup like a man possessed when he eventually pronounced his find. "It's ok George," I said hastily. "I think it's coming off now!"

"Why don't ye just send it back?" he suggested calmly, causing me to immediately stop the frantic cleaning and look up at him.

"Huh?' was all I could reply. I didn't understand. I thought he was going to offer me some dodgy polishing cream or something, not make a normal suggestion that I return the mug of tea! I quickly scanned his hands but saw nothing. No sachets of powder or bottles of secret potion that carried the skull and crossbones motif warning people of danger; nothing!

"Just send it back!" he repeated and then added. "Or d'ye like having friction burns on your fingers?"

I felt my face reddening a little. "Well ... I, erm ... Yes, I might just do that!" I stammered uncomfortably. The thing was, I had totally mis-read George's pocket searching antics and like a plonker, had imagined the worse. And what's more, I had no doubts that George knew this too! Hence my rapid *exit stage left* to go and change my drink!

I returned to the table a couple of minutes later with a fresh mug of tea for myself and a rather large chocolate éclair for George ... kind of a silent conscience clearer if you like?

George's eyes lit up when I placed the cake in front of him. "Well, Ah was watching ma figure," he joked. "But Ah suppose it can wait until tomorrow!"

As I resumed my seat, I saw an envelope sitting on the table in front of me. From its faded colour and blackened crease marks, where it had been folded and re-folded time again, I could tell that it was quite old and immediately

---

104

became intrigued. "Hello, what's this?" I asked picking up the fragile paper packet and examining it more closely.

"It's what Ah wanted tae show you," George replied. "It's the letter that Patterson gave Lilly after he hud read the Will!"

I looked up at George. "From Isaac?" I asked enthusiastically.

"Aye," he answered. I turned the envelope slowly in my hands and unfolded it to reveal the single word on its front face ... *Lilly*.

I glanced across at George again who simply smiled back at me. "Ok if I ...?" I started, gesturing towards it.

"Aye, be ma guest," he consented.

I studied the envelope again and eventually (yet carefully) extracted the letter from inside, handling it with the same consideration that might be applied to an historic document from the archives of the British Library. No, it wasn't an ancient artefact or a page from the Doomsday Book, but it was a piece of this man's history. At some point in George's life, that letter had been held by the two people that had meant so much to him and because of that, I intended to treat it with respect!

The pages had yellowed over the years and emitted an unusually sweet yet musty aroma that reminded me of a museum. In some places, pieces of sticky tape had been used to cull the progression of tears in the paper, like plasters covering small cuts to the skin. But this too had suffered from the effects of time and had all but lost its adhesiveness, allowing the unhealed wounds of the sheets to open once more and bleed into the faded ink of the handwritten text.

For some reason, I had imagined that the written work of an old fisherman, who was probably more akin to hauling nets than penning a letter, would have been little more than an illegible scrawl. But I couldn't have been more wrong as I marvelled at the beautifully scribed words on the paper. It put me in mind of what an original Charles Dickens novel might have looked like; intricate text that had been carefully applied to each leaf with the skilful stroke of a fountain pen. As I prepared to read the letter, I suddenly felt myself being transported back in time as the image of an aged Scot, sitting at an old writing bureau, dominated my mind's eye. It was a surreal and hypnotic feeling yet it seemed to be the most natural and fitting place for my subconscious to reside at that particular moment. I didn't resist, I read on.

My Dearest Lilly ...

###

Lilly McBride

16

On 27th March 1928 both Angus McBride and Isaac Andrews became very proud men yet only Angus would be able to openly display his pride as he publicly announced the birth of his beautiful daughter, Lilly.

Isaac had never seen The Jolly Piper as busy as it was on the night of Lilly's birth, though he put this down more to the landlord's offer of free drinks rather than the patron's wish to share in Angus's excitement; nothing more fickle than a parched Scot getting drinks on the house, he thought.

Isaac had seen and heard enough. He finished his drink and set his glass down, wanting to tell the whole sorry crowd that Lilly was his and not Angus's. But he wouldn't. He would quietly leave the pub, head home and find solace in a bottle of whisky before passing out.

As he walked along the quiet street, agonising over the fact that he had become an unaccredited father whilst having to watch another man bask in a joy that should have been his, he was surprised to hear the voice of Angus calling after him and turned round to see the man almost running towards him. For some inexplicable reason, he imagined that Angus now knew everything about the affair with Margaret and was coming to confront him. Isaac found himself adapting a defensive stance that he had done so many times in the boxing ring; his body bladed, his chin slightly lowered and though his arms were by his side, he had naturally clenched his fists contemplating a pre-emptive strike. But then logic, coupled with the smile he could see on Angus's face as he approached, made him relax a little ... though not completely.

"Why ye leaving?" Angus asked, once he had caught up with Isaac. "Ah didnae think ye would turn down a free bar!" Isaac smiled, wanting to tell him exactly why he had left. Fortunately, this train of thought was quickly interrupted by Angus's continuance. "Listen," he said. "Ah wanted tae ask ye something but Ah huvnae had the chance, what with everything that's been goin' on!"

"Aye, it's been an eventful day for ye," Isaac agreed. "And Ah'm pleased for ye an' Margaret, Ah really am!" The last comment was a lie. He wasn't pleased in the slightest. If anything, he was envious of the family that Angus now had and bitterly thought that it should have been him, not this man before him that was publicly rejoicing the birth of *his* daughter. At that moment in time, Isaac wanted to knock the contented smile off Angus's face.

"Thanks Isaac. Ah know ye are," Angus replied. "Which is why Ah want tae ask ye something important!" Isaac frowned. "Don't look so worried," Angus continued. "But ye can say no if ye don't want tae ... Ah mean, Ah wullnae take it the wrong way but if ..."

"Spit it oot man!" Isaac interrupted.

"Aye, of course," Angus replied. "Well, Ah would be honoured if ye would consider being Lilly's Godparent? But only if ye want tae of course?"

Isaac was taken aback by the sudden and unexpected request and for a short while, found himself speechless. "And what does Margaret say aboot that?" he finally asked.

"Tae tell ye the truth, it was her idea!" Angus replied. "But as Ah couldnae think of anyone better, Ah had tae agree!" he added, laughing.

Isaac smiled back and though he knew his answer straight away, he told Angus that it was a decision not to be taken lightly and that he needed time to consider such a responsibility. He actually wanted to say yes there and then, but a strong feeling that over enthusiasm might arouse some suspicion from Angus, caused him to delay his response and wait over a week before he finally accepted. Angus was pleased ... Margaret more so.

###

From a very early age, Lilly showed an intellect beyond her years and when she finally started school, she displayed an overwhelming aptitude for learning and subsequently excelled in every subject. From the age of eight, she had two ambitions in life. The first was to be a teacher and she would often be seen educating her classroom of dolls and bears in the front parlour in a style that was befitting somebody three times her age; organised, knowledgeable and strangely, firm but fair.

The second of her ambitions worried her mother. Not because she thought (or rather hoped) that it would ever happen but more because she felt that her wish to work on a sea trawler was a gene most definitely inherited from her real father. In fact, Lilly began to spend more and more time at the harbour, talking with her godfather and the other fisherman and loved to help clean the decks whenever The Pearl of Good Hope was moored. Margaret had secretly asked Isaac to discourage Lilly from her new found interest so that questions (however innocent) wouldn't be raised and cause suspicion in Angus. Isaac agreed to do his best though it didn't help matters when, at nine years old, Lilly decided to stow away on his boat.

Isaac's decision was hard. He loved Lilly more than life itself and having her around the harbour so often, meant the world to him. But he knew that she was better than that and to waste such obvious intelligence on a future of hauling nets and cleaning out fish guts, was not the path he wanted to see his daughter travel. So as gently and persuasively as he could, he enforced Margaret's request and set about steering Lilly's ambitions in a different direction.

Thus, over the following years, Lilly was weaned off her love of sea fishing. She continued to excel at her school work and with numerous citations from her teachers and constantly outstanding exam results, it came as no surprise when she was accepted at college and, later, at Edinburgh University to train as a teacher.

Isaac looked on proudly as she blossomed into a beautiful young lady and though her visits to the harbour became less frequent, she would always call on him whenever she had the chance, whether it was for advice or just a simple chat. Though Lilly never said, she somehow felt a lot closer to Isaac than she did Angus. Not that she didn't love Angus, she did. But with Isaac, she always felt safe and that his interest in her was true and unconditional ... like a father should be, she thought. It was a shame that Angus didn't display the same fatherly qualities ... she also thought.

On 27th March 1946, Lilly became eighteen years of age. To celebrate this, a private party had been arranged at The Jolly Piper for later that evening. It was supposed to have been a surprise, but she accidentally overheard her mum talking about it the night before. "Will Uncle Isaac be there?" was Lilly's first comment after her initial excitement had died down.

"Ah think so," her mother replied with a smile. "He certainly knows about it!"

That wasn't enough for Lilly. She needed to know for definite. She loved her godfather and without him she knew that the party wouldn't be as enjoyable. And so, on the morning of her birthday, she rose at the crack of dawn and ran down to the harbour where she knew Isaac would be preparing for the day's fishing expedition,

"An' what's ma little star doing up so early?" Isaac asked as soon as he saw her.

"Well," Lilly began, with a large smile on her face. "I wanted to make sure that you are coming tonight."

"And where would that be?" Isaac asked, knowing all too well what she meant.

"My party of course ... and don't pretend you don't know!"

Isaac smiled. "A party y'say? An' what would that be for?" he teased.

Lilly sighed, jumped onto the deck of the boat and stood in front of Isaac with her hands on her hips and a playfully stern look on her face. "And don't try to pretend that you don't know what day it is today either!"

Isaac laughed out loud. "Ye know me too well Missy," he said. "Now give me a big hug, birthday girl!"

Lilly threw her arms around Isaac and he held her with an embrace that is solely reserved for fathers and their daughters. "So you'll be coming to my party then?" she asked as they finally released each other.

"Ah widnae miss it for the world!" Isaac replied. "Now get off ma boat, Ah've work tae do!"

Lilly smiled and kissed him on the cheek. "Thank you," she whispered, before climbing back onto the harbour wall and walking away.

Isaac watched her for a few moments before he rushed to the relative privacy of the boat's bridge. The deck hands

would be arriving soon and it really wouldn't do for them to
see him weeping like this.

Lilly walked slowly back along the harbour wall,
smiling. She turned back to wave at Isaac, but she could see
that he had his back to her as he climbed up the steps that led
to the bridge of his boat. The sun was just starting to come up
on what promised to be a beautiful day so she decided to sit a
while and watch Isaac's boat set out to sea. As she sat there
letting the slight, fresh breeze wash over her, a few men,
young and old, passed by her. "Morning Lilly," some said.
"Happy birthday Lilly," all said. Lilly knew each and every
one of them by name; after all, she had mingled with her
godfather's deck hands for most of her life both at the harbour
and in her father's pub.

She acknowledged them all like they were family,
sharing a hug and a joke with most before watching them head
off towards The Pearl of Good Hope. A few minutes went by
before another young man walked past and then stopped only a
few feet in front of her, only this time, Lilly had no idea who
he was. She guessed that he was about the same age as she
was, with thick, unkempt hair that made him look quite
attractive in a funny kind of way. But, given his slim build and
relatively clean clothes, she also thought that he didn't look too
much like a fisherman. *'Probably somebody else trying to
avoid National Service!'* she mused cynically. She couldn't
help but smile when he suddenly produced a piece of paper
from his pocket that she immediately recognised as being an
interim worker's docket supplied by the Harbour Master.
'Knew it!' she thought smugly.

Lilly watched the stranger with mild amusement as he
stood there looking from the docket to the numerous moored
boats and then back again, in rapid succession. He looked like
a little boy lost and though Lilly could have probably helped
him with locating the boat he was searching for straight away,

she found this display of vulnerability quite endearing. When she had watched him suffer for long enough, she finally spoke. "Are ye looking for a particular boat?"

The stranger jumped slightly and quickly turned around. In the relative darkness of the early morning, he hadn't seen the female sat behind him and even now, had to squint to try and focus on the form encased in shadow. Lilly, however, had no problem in seeing the stranger as the rising sun, coupled with the glow of the gas lamp he was stood next to, lit him up like a beacon. If she had any doubts about his attractive features from his side profile, she certainly didn't have any now. He quite took her breath away.

"Sorry, Ah didnae see y' there!" he exclaimed.

"Clearly!" Lilly replied nonchalantly. She hoped he couldn't hear her heart, which was suddenly beating very fast.

"Aye ... right!" the man said, still trying to focus on the owner of the voice. "Ah'm looking for ... " he stopped and glanced down at his docket to check the name. "The Pearl of Good Hope!" he continued, before looking back towards Lilly.

Lilly gasped, though thankfully not loud enough for the man to hear. She wanted to tell him that her godfather owned that boat and that she would personally escort him to it if he liked? ... and that her father owned The Jolly Piper pub, if he would like to meet her there later maybe, for a drink? And my name is Lilly, what's yours? ... but she didn't. All she could manage to do was point in the direction of Isaac's trawler and blurt out its location. And before she could re-compose herself, the man was heading off, double time, towards the boat.

Not until she spoke with Isaac later that evening at her party (in her best *matter of fact, not really that interested* voice) did she discover that the man's name was George. According to Isaac, he seemed a nice enough lad ... a little touchy mind ... but there was no doubt that he worked hard enough. And from what he could tell, George wasn't married

---

115

and didn't even have a girlfriend. "No' that ye would be interested in that!" he concluded with a wink and a wry smirk.

"Of course not!" Lilly replied a little too quickly. "Why should Ah be?" Isaac simply raised his eyebrows and grinned at Lilly. "What?" she demanded. But before Isaac could reply, she shook her head, tutted and quickly scurried off hoping that her flushed face and developing smile hadn't given her true feelings away.

Shortly after her eighteenth birthday, Lilly went away to Edinburgh to study for her vocation as a teacher.

Although the intensive work posed no real problems for her, Lilly struggled with being apart from her family. She dearly missed her parents and Isaac during her time away and though the regular letter writing and occasional trip home during the holidays had helped ease the feeling of loneliness, it was no substitute for being permanently close to them. So, after a year had passed, she came to the decision that she would complete her studies at a university closer to home. Her grades for that year had been exemplary and with a promised letter of recommendation from her tutor, transferring to a different campus wouldn't be too difficult.

On one of the few weekends that Lilly didn't have a mountain of essays to write or books to study, she returned home to inform her parents (and Isaac of course) of her plans. Her mother and godfather were delighted that she was *coming home* whereas her father was a little more reserved. "Will it no' interfere with your studies wi' all the distractions about?" he asked. Lilly had reminded him that in their town, there was little to distract her ... but that was before she found herself lending a hand in her dad's pub later that evening and saw George walk in ... suddenly, she wasn't so sure.

17

Angus wasn't one to hide his dis-approval, so when Lilly told him and her mother that she was attracted to George, he didn't hold back. "Ye've far more important things to be thinking aboot than daydreaming o'er some bloody no hope fisherman!"

"What's wrong with fishermen?" Lilly asked.

"They're classless, moral-less an' most of them huvnae a pot tae piss in an' Ah'll nay huv any daughter of mine wasting her life on that sort!"

"That sort?" Lilly exclaimed sharply, becoming angry. "You don't seem to mind 'that sort' when they're filling the cash till in your pub! ... whose moral-less now?"

Angus stood up from his seat, banging his hand hard on the table so that both Lilly and her mother flinched. "Ye mind your tongue young lady!" He shouted. "Ah take their money to provide for this family an' keep a roof over our heads. And in case ye huv forgotten, it pays towards your education ye ungrateful little ...!"

"Angus!" Margaret reproached sharply.

Angus glared at his wife. He would have said something to her had Lilly not spoken first. "Then maybe Ah should give up my education if it's such a burden to you!" she said, her voice beginning to crack as she fought back tears.

Angus turned to face her again. "What? So ye can waste your life on a fish gutter? Well Ah'll no' allow it!"

"Ah'm eighteen years old, how can you not allow it?"

"Because Ah'm your father!" Angus replied, his voice becoming louder. "An' whilst ye are living under ma roof, ye will follow ma rules!"

"Then maybe Ah should move out!" Lilly shouted as she stood up, tears now rolling down her cheeks.

"Aye, maybe ye should! Let's see how long ye last with half an education and no money!"

"Ah don't need your money ... Ah'll get a job!"

"What as? A docker's whore!"

"Enough!" Margaret shouted, getting to her own feet. Now it was her turn to scowl at Angus. "Lilly, go to your room!" she instructed, not taking her eyes off her husband. Lilly stood fast at the table, open-mouthed, stunned by her father's comment. "Now!" her mother instructed again. Lilly jumped at the raised voice and looked at her mum hoping for some words of comfort. When none came, she ran off to her room sobbing heavily.

"Thanks for your support!" Angus snorted, sarcastically.

"If she leaves," Margaret began, as if her husband had said nothing. "Then Ah'll be leaving with her!"

Angus stared at his wife in dis-belief. "An' ye think it's okay for her tae speak to me like that?" he gasped.

"No," Margaret conceded. "But neither do Ah think ye should belittle your daughter!" Angus sighed as Margaret continued. "She's no longer a child Angus, she's a grown woman and if nothing else, you should know that she's very strong willed!"

"Ah don't want tae see her throw her life away on some ... " Angus began.

"On some what?" Margaret interrupted. "Some young man that she's seen once and has taken a fancy too. She's no' even been out with the lad and you've imagined that her life is over, married off with no future. Not everybody sacrifices their dreams like ...!" Margaret suddenly checked herself, realising what she had said.

"Like what?" Angus asked, scowling. "Like you? Is that what ye were going t'say?" Margaret bowed her head and remained silent. "Well Ah'm sorry tae have wasted your life," He added quietly.

"You haven't wasted my life Angus," Margaret said after a moments pause. "Ah chose my path and Ah'm happy with it!" Angus looked up at Margaret as she moved towards him and took hold of his hand. "Ah just sometimes wish that Ah ... we ... hud been more adventurous ...!"

"Oh," Angus interjected. "So ye're sayin' Ah'm boring?"

"No," Margaret answered with a smile. "Ah'm saying that sometimes, we could huv been ... well ... more spontaneous, more free spirited perhaps!"

"Jesus woman, ye'll huv us living in a commune next, drinking tea made oot o' dandelions and growing long hair!" He saw Margaret glance towards his receding hairline and smiled. "Well, maybe no' the long hair bit!" he added.

Margaret chuckled and took hold of Angus's other hand, pulling him closer as she did. "Lilly's a sensible girl Angus," she began. "But whatever path she decides to take, we must support her ... both of us ... or risk losing her!"

Angus sighed and hugged his wife. "Aye, Ah suppose ye're right," he said quietly. "But Ah only want what's best for ma girls ... as stubborn as ye both are!" Margaret pulled away slightly, looked at Angus with a feigned look of shock and quickly administered a playful smack to his arm. Angus yelped with an equally feigned display of pain causing them both to chuckle. When Margaret sat back down Angus followed suit and looked intensely at his wife. "Now," he continued, with a more serious tone in his voice. "What do we know aboot this George fella?"

The courtship period between George and Lilly was relatively short and after only a few months, he knew that this was the girl he wanted to spend the rest of his life with. When he finally mustered up enough courage to propose, Lilly accepted.

"If Ah knew it was going to be that easy," George said, holding her close. "Ah'd huv asked ye weeks ago!"

Lilly looked up at him and smiled. "It took you long enough!" she teased. "Ah'd huv said yes after our first date!"

18

"Do ye love him?"

"Yes Ah do!"

"And does he love you?"

"Yes ... well, he says that he does ... and Ah believe him!"

"Then nothing or nobody else should matter!"

Lilly frowned and let out a sigh. She knew that Isaac was right. If only her father had the same attitude.

"Listen tae me," Isaac said, taking hold of Lilly's hand. "Your father is jus' being protective. And, if truth be told, Ah suspect he's a wee bit scared!"

"Scared? Scared of what?" Lilly asked. "Of George?"

"No' of George exactly but the fact that he is taking his daughter away!"

"But we won't be leaving the town!"

Isaac laughed. "It doesnae matter where ye go," he said. "It's the fact that he can no longer look after you and has tae pass that responsibility over tae another man!"

"Well he has no reason to worry ... And Ah can look after myself thank you very much!"

Isaac laughed for a second time and patted Lilly's hand. "Aye lassie, Ah'm sure ye can!" he started. "But fathers want the best for their daughters and we'll always think that no other man is good enough for them!"

Lilly frowned again. "What do you mean 'we'? You're not a father!"

"Eh?"

"You said, *we'll* always think that no man is good enough ... but you huvnae got a daughter?" Isaac felt himself redden as he realised what he had said. A slip of the tongue that Lilly, as sharp as ever, had quickly picked up on. He began to panic a little, wondering how he could explain himself without rousing suspicion. Thankfully, it was Lilly that saved him from further despair. "Although you might as well be my father," she continued. "At least you listen!"

"He'll come round eventually," Isaac added quickly, thankful of the reprieve. "An' for what it's worth, Ah think George is a good man, so ye'd huv ma blessin' ... if ye were ma daughter that is!"

Lilly smiled and then hugged Isaac. "Thank you," she said. "That's worth more than you know!"

When Lilly was leaving, Isaac saw her to his front door, kissed her on the cheek and then stood and watched as she walked away. Once she was out of sight, he went back indoors and took a seat at his writing bureau. He had been sat there for almost an hour contemplating a very important decision he felt he had to make. Convinced he was doing the right thing, he placed some fresh writing paper in front of himself, recharged his ink pen and began to write ... *My Dearest Lilly.*

###

19

After a few years of marriage, nobody could say that George and Lilly weren't the perfect couple, though a few Small-minded gossipmongers found it strange that Lilly had not yet borne a child; after all, was that not the lawful duty of a wife?

"If it's meant to be," Margaret had told her daughter. "Then it will happen when the Good Lord decides, no' on the say so of some narrow minded fish wives!"

Isaac was of the same opinion as Margaret ... as was George, as were all of Lilly's friends ... but it was clear, from the occasional comment, usually encouraged by alcohol, that her father was firmly in the same school as the *fish wives*.

George was furious when he heard how Angus had upset Lilly with his ale-loosened mouth and wanted to help him shut it. Only the insistence of his wife had stopped him from marching round to The Jolly Piper pub to *have a word* with Angus, though he was in no doubt that the opportunity to educate his father-in-law would present itself again in the future.

"Ah married you tae be with you," George had said, once calm had been restored. "An' whether we huv none or a hundred bairns, nothing will change that! ... It's ye Ah love Lilly, no' the opinion of fools!"

As the years went by, so the biological clock of Lilly faded like an old photograph. The words of comfort and the display of undeniable love from George did little to convince Lilly that she hadn't let him down but in time, she grew to accept that there would be no addition to the Bell family, however much she wanted it.

###

When George was in work, times were hard but manageable. When he wasn't, it was a financial nightmare to make ends meet. Lilly's meagre wage as a teacher didn't go very far and it was only with the kind help of Isaac that they could actually put food on the table. Lilly found it strange that this benevolence hadn't been offered by her own father though she suspected that the well publicised altercation between him and George had put paid to that.

"He could always come back tae work with me," Isaac had offered, though they both knew that George would never entertain that proposal. But why? Neither of them really knew and whenever Lilly asked George about the reason he had left The Pearl of Good Hope in the first place, he would always offer some feeble excuse about seasickness or just clam up completely.

George had only ever gotten temporary jobs since leaving the fishing industry (not much call for an uneducated man that had *dodged the draft*) and even they had become increasingly more difficult to find as recruiting *younger* men evolved as the new fashion for forward thinking employers. And so it was, that from mid 1966, George would remain unemployed for over three years bringing about the hardest period of their marriage yet. Angus thrived on this believing that, sooner or later, the relationship would end and he would see the return of his daughter desperate to sever ties with that no-hoper of a husband. What he didn't bank on was the fact that the situation seemed to make them even more inseparable, bonding them closer in a way that Angus loathed.

"She'll soon see that's she's better off wi' oot that good fae nothin'!" he had pointed out to Margaret on several occasions. And when George eventually found work in the winter of 1969, the only change to Angus's bitter remark was, "Ah'll give it three weeks until he's oot on his arse again ... and then she'll see that she's better off wi' oot that good fae nothin!"

December 1969 was both the worst and the best time in Lilly's life. George had a job that promised to be more permanent that temporary, whilst she had been recommended to become deputy head teacher at the school where she worked. She was even planning for Christmas when she knew she would be giving George his best present ever.

But a dark cloud had quickly muddied the waters of good fortune the day that Isaac passed away. News of the inheritance was as surprising as it was welcomed but the revelation that Mr Patterson had also imparted during the reading of Isaac's will had left Lilly feeling numb.

And now she sat in her lounge staring at an unopened letter on her lap. A letter from Isaac addressed to her ... his daughter. She sensed that George was hovering somewhere behind her and knew that he would have many words of comfort to offer, given the chance. But she didn't want to speak; she doubted that she could of even if she had wanted to. What she did want was to scream, to cry, to laugh, to go back in time, to shout at Isaac, to hug Isaac and to hear him say, "Ah'm your dad Lilly!" ... but she couldn't.

None of it made any sense. Maybe the letter would make it clear but there again, what was there to make clear? What could it possibly say that she didn't already know? ... 'Dear Lilly, I'm your father, enjoy the money!"? ... maybe she should just burn it and have done.

Tears rolled down Lilly's cheeks as she fought back the bitterness that tried to take a hold of her emotions. She picked up the letter and turned it over in her hands several times before finally deciding that the man whom she had cherished for all these years had a right to be heard ... she owed him that at least.

She carefully unsealed the envelope, removed the letter from within and began to read ... *My Dearest Lilly.*

20

I don't think that I have ever had to face anything so hard as writing this letter to you and heaven only knows where I should begin.

I hope that you can forgive my cowardice, as I know that if you are reading this letter, then I have passed away and Mr Patterson has handed it to you. You will have also discovered that you are my daughter and no words that I write now can tell you how sorry I am for the way the truth was revealed. I am not usually one to shy away from confrontation but I could not bring myself to tell you what lay heavy on my heart whilst I lived, for fear of spending my waking days without your love. You mean the world to me Lilly and I could not risk your happiness or losing you for the sake of a self-indulgent clearing of conscience!

The day I wrote this letter, you had just been to see me. It was just after George had asked for your hand in marriage. Do you remember? ...

Lilly nodded and smiled, wiping her eyes before she continued to read.

...you were filled with so much excitement and love as you talked about your future that it reminded me of a time when I too felt the same way. It was the day that your mother told me that she was expecting a child ... my child. I was breathless with joy. I was going to be a father and I wanted to shout it from the rooftops!

I loved your mother with all my heart and would have given my life to protect and care for her and my child. But what we had done was wrong and we both knew that she would have to remain with Angus. Love is a powerful thing Lilly but it couldn't have offered the security that your mother needed to bring a child into the world and so I had to let her go. I hope that you can understand why I did what I did but know that I have regretted that decision for all of my life.

I cannot tell you how sorry I am for all the years of deceit and for allowing you to believe that Angus was your natural father. God knows I wanted to tell you every time I saw you but what purpose would it have served? ... Only upset and anger I feel.

Please do not think ill of your mother for my sins of the past. She only ever wanted what was best for you and nobody, neither Angus, nor I would have come close to receiving the amount of love she has for you. Personally, I will be forever indebted to her for bringing the most beautiful thing into this world and allowing me to become your godfather ... I hope that I at least, succeeded in that role?

And so, my darling Lilly, I feel I have said all that I

need to say other than to thank you for being the most wonderful daughter a man could ever hope to have and for allowing me to share your life. You made me proud every single day and I am honoured (if only secretly) to have been your dad.

I hope that you can find it in your heart to forgive an old fool's stupidity and selfishness but I will understand if this is too much to ask.

My only true wish is for you to be happy!

Forever in my heart.

Your loving father

Isaac x

PS ... George will make a fine husband.

After reading the letter for a second time, Lilly folded the paper in half and returned it to the envelope, her eyes stinging from the tears that were still falling. Deep down, she had suspected that Isaac and her mother had had a romantic history but finding out that she was his daughter after his death had hit Lilly hard. Not because he was her father but because she hadn't been given the opportunity to be his daughter. She loved Isaac and always would and there was no question that she forgave him. Yet his sudden and unexpected death had denied her the chance to tell him the one thing she had waited all her life to share with him ...

She jumped slightly as George appeared by her side and placed a hand on her shoulder. "You ok?" he asked.

Staring at George through watery eyes, she replied. "No, not really!" her lips quivering as she spoke. George leant down and took his wife in his arms, holding her tightly as she wept into his chest. He felt powerless and ashamed ... ashamed that he had known Isaac's secret for some time but had kept it to himself.

As if sensing his guilt, Lilly pulled away, composed herself and gave him a long stare that made him swallow with anxiety. And then she said something so totally unexpected that it almost knocked George off his feet. "You know what upsets me the most?" she asked rhetorically. George could only shake his head. "It's the fact that I can't tell him what I know he'd been longing to hear!" she paused again.

"And what's that?" George encouraged quietly.

Lilly took hold of his hand and smiled. "That we are going to be parents!"

21

I almost choked to death on my tea when George revealed that particular snippet of his life. "Ye ok son?" he asked casually, as he returned the re-folded letter to his pocket. I held up my hand and flicked my fingers in a rapid, semi-wave movement; the internationally accepted signal that I'd live ... given a minute or two.

I looked at George through streaming eyes and attempted to speak. But those annoying little after-shock coughs, that always develop when you've saturated your lungs, put paid to that for a short while. When I eventually recovered, George was buttoning up his coat (or rather the last three remaining buttons on his coat) as if he was getting ready to leave.

"You're not going now are you?" I asked, hoping that he was just cold ... bizarre I know.

"Aye," he replied. "Ah've things tae do!"

'Like what for Christ's sake?' I thought impatiently. *'You're homeless!'* "But I wanted to know about Lilly being pregnant," I continued with the tone of an over enthusiastic child. "And how you felt, knowing that you were going to become a father after all those years and ... "

"No' jus' now!" he cut in with a noticeable tone of insistence. He stood up quickly, adjusted his attire and began to walk out, leaving me sitting there with a feeling of confused frustration. He then he stopped, mid exit, just beyond my shoulder. I turned and looked up at him but remained silent. He was staring straight ahead, focused on something beyond the cafe and most definitely beyond the present time; no doubt back into another era. And then he turned to me with the same look of sorrow in his eyes that I had often seen during our times together. "Y' know son?" he began softly. "No' everything in life turns oot fae the best!" He held me in his stare for a moment and then sighed. "See ye soon laddie!"

I watched him leave, wondering why he looked so sad after telling me about what really should have been a (if not thee) highlight of his life ... Two weeks later, I found out why.

###

22

December 1969 ... George swayed a little as he tried to take in what he had just been told. He let go of Lilly's hand and sat (or rather fell) into a chair opposite his wife, a million questions flying around inside his head. Lilly tried to judge his reaction but couldn't fathom out whether he was pleased or not.

She waited until he spoke, allowing him to gather his thoughts ... God knows it was a big thing to take in.

"So," he finally began. "Ye're tellin' me that ye're pregnant?" Lilly nodded her head, adding a slight smile. "An' we're huving a bairn?" he added.

"That's normally what happens when ye're pregnant!" Lilly regretted the reply as soon as she had made it ... probably not the best time for sarcasm.

"Aye, aye, of course it does, aye," George continued, oblivious to it. He paused for a moment, rubbed his face with his hands and then looked back at Lilly. "But how did? ... Ah mean, when did? ... Ah mean ... pregnant ye say?"

"Are ye alright George?" Lilly asked feeling a little concerned.

"Alright? Aye, aye. Ah'm ... " His voice suddenly trailed off and he bowed his head causing Lilly to get up from her chair and go across to him. George looked up at his wife just as tears began to track down his cheeks. Lilly gasped and dropped to her knees, cupping her husband's large face in her small hands.

"Oh George darling," she began, wiping the tears from his weathered skin with her delicate fingers. "Ah'm so sorry, please don't cry!"

George frowned. "What are ye sorry fae?"

"For telling you," Lilly replied. "Ah thought ye'd be pleased!"

George moved Lilly away slightly, holding her at arms length. "Pleased?" he said, looking at her intently. "Ah'm no pleased Lilly!" he continued. "Ah'm bloody ecstatic!"

27th March 1970 was Lilly's forty-second birthday and she couldn't have been happier. Her regular check up at the doctors that morning had shown that all was well with her pregnancy (now in its third month) and though Doctor McKay had noted that her blood pressure was a little high, he didn't feel there was too much to be concerned about at this stage. "Just make sure ye huv plenty of rest Lillian," he advised, placing a stethoscope around his neck. "Huving a child at your age is no' an easy task and judging by the size of ye now ..." he ran his hand over her Lilly's tummy. "... ye are going tae need all your strength to deliver this one into the world!"

Lilly smiled and ran her own hands gently across her bump. "Anyway," she began with a slight frown. "I'm not that old. I feel like I'm in my twenties!"

Doctor McKay grimaced. "Ah didnae say you were old Lillian, Ah just meant ... "

"Ah know doctor," Lilly interjected. "Ah was jus' teasing. And Ah promise to take things easy!"

Lilly had decided not to tell George about her high blood pressure. After all, there was no point in worrying the man over something that even the Doctor didn't seem too concerned about.

Lilly knew that George would be working overtime (though Heaven only knew why, it's not like they needed the money anymore) and he had suggested that she visit her parents that afternoon and meet him at Isaac's house around six pm later that evening.

"Working, on my birthday?" she had said to her husband. "Oh, that's nice! ... and why Isaac's house?" she finished, with a frown.

"Ah'm sorry Lilly," George had replied. "But Ah don't want to let work down. They've been good tae me over the months. And apparently ..." he went on to explain. "There's a wee leak in Isaac's gutter that needs looking at, so that's why

Ah said tae meet there. Then we could go for a drink afterwards maybe? ... tae celebrate your day?"

Lilly sighed. "There won't be much left of my day at this rate," she sulked. "And Ah don't see why you have to work anymore either. Isaac left us enough money and we should enjoy it now ... together ... while we're still young enough!"

"Says you, Miss Deputy Head Teacher," George countered with a smile. "The school will still run withoot ye if ye left y' know? ... and they wullnae huv to spend money on widening the doors!"

Lilly gasped. George laughed and left the room just in time to avoid being hit by a flying cushion. He then popped his head back around the door and smiled at his wife. "But Ah still love you, birthday girl!" he added, before leaving once again.

Lilly smiled at the conversation she and George had had earlier that morning and was still smiling when she entered her mum and dad's house.

"Somebody looks happy!" Margaret exclaimed, when she saw her daughter.

"That's because Ah am!" Lilly replied, as she kissed then hugged her mum.

"Happy birthday darling," Margaret said, before pulling away slightly and placing a hand on Lilly's tummy. "And how's ma wee grandchild doing?"

"Well, Doctor McKay said that everything was going well," Lilly replied.

Margaret frowned at her daughter and sat down. "But?" she probed.

Lilly thought about lying to her mum but she knew that it would be pointless. "He said that my blood pressure was a little high," she replied, and then quickly added. "But he said it was nothing to worry about as long as Ah take things easy!"

"Well, Ah hope ye take his advice," Margaret said sternly. "Ah know how stubborn ye can be when ye are told tae do something ye donae want to do, but this is important!"

"Ah know mum and Ah will take things easy, Ah promise!"

"And what about school? Huv ye spoken to them about leaving yet?" Margaret quizzed.

"Not yet but Ah ..."

"Och, there ye go," Margaret interrupted. " Not yet, y' say ... You cannae take things easy if ye're stood on your feet all day teaching! Doctor McKay knows what ..."

"Mum, mum. Ah know!" Lilly cut in. "But Ah only found out today didn't Ah? Ah'll sort it out ... stop worrying!"

"When?"

"Soon. Ah promise!"

Margaret glared at her daughter for a moment and then sighed. "Aye. Well make sure ye do!" She got up from her chair and smiled. "Now. Why don't Ah make us a nice cup of tea and we can talk about baby names again?"

Lilly smiled and nodded. As her mother toddled off into the kitchen, she couldn't help but wonder where Angus was on her birthday. But then she thought about Isaac.

"Well," George began. "Ah best get back and sort things oot ... thanks for listening!" He climbed up onto the harbour wall and turned to face The Pearl of Good Hope. An unexpected yet pleasant breeze washed over him. He breathed the air deep into his lungs then exhaled slowly. Checking that nobody else was around, he turned back towards the trawler and whispered. "Ah'll speak to ye soon Isaac!" He then gave a

133

casual salute and walked away, the old boat creaking to the rhythm of the sea.

Lilly didn't find her mother's decision to walk with her to Isaac's the least bit unusual. In fact, she welcomed the idea as it meant that they could continue their conversation about Mary McDonald; a colourful local woman whose explicit business venture had brought about a recent visit from the police ... nothing like good gossip to help along an otherwise monotonous walk. But when they arrived at the house, she frowned slightly. It looked a little different from the last time she had seen it nearly 3 months ago; fresher, neater somehow. And she could have sworn that she saw Angus at one of the windows ... only very briefly perhaps, but still.

"Are you ok darling?" her mother asked, seeing the look on her daughters face.

Lilly turned towards Margaret, a slight smile on her face. "Ah think something's going on here!" she replied before quickly advancing towards the front door. As she entered the house, she jumped at the resounding cry of "Surprise!" from the small gathering of family and friends stood inside waiting on her arrival. The initial look of shock was replaced by a large smile as the group began to sing *Happy Birthday* and George came forward to hug her. She kissed George just before the tears fell from her eyes but then pulled away and playfully smacked his chest. "How did you manage to arrange all this? And when did you find the time? You're always at work!"

"Well," George began with a smile. "Ah think Ah huv a wee confession tae make!"

134

The birthday surprise had turned out well and everybody appeared to be having a good time. Lilly was overjoyed (and completely taken aback) when George eventually revealed his confession. She had no idea that he had actually left his job at the beginning of January that year and had secretly set about renovating Isaac's former home so that they could take up residence in time for the birth of their child. She had no idea that her mother had helped organise the surprise party without so much as a hint as to what was going on ... unlike her eighteenth she thought ... but thankfully, she also had no idea of the conversation that George and Angus were now having out in the garden.

"You've done well here George," Angus said, moving his arm towards the house in a clumsy sweeping motion that made some of the beer fly out of the glass he was holding. George didn't reply but watched closely as his intoxicated father-in-law attempted to wipe some of the spilt drink off his hand. "Aye, you've done well," he repeated in more of a mutter to himself. Giving up on the wet hand, Angus stared down at the ground, swaying slightly. He glanced at George as if he was about to say something but then thought better of it ... or had lost his nerve. He then gave the faintest of smiles and looked back down at the ground.

George knew exactly what Angus was going to ask him but wanted to let him suffer the indignity of trying a little while longer. He despised this man immensely but for the sake of Lilly had learned to tolerate him. He knew that the hate was reciprocated too and wasn't fooled in the slightest by Angus's unusual show of friendliness over the past few months; a friendliness that had started (by the strangest of coincidences) just after the news that George and Lilly had been the beneficiaries of Isaac's will. Angus had told Lilly that it was time for him to bury the hatchet with George for the sake of the unborn child and she had fallen for the spiel. George hadn't, seeing right through the false sentiments, though had agreed to try and get along with Angus nonetheless ... not for the sake of his unborn child, for the sake of his wife.

George knew that Angus had asked Lilly for money on more than a few occasions, stating that pub had come up against some minor cash flow problems. "This is just a temporary loan you understand?" he had said to her on receipt of the first hand out. "I will pay you back every penny just as soon as things turn around!" Lilly had dismissed this stating that she was more than happy to help him out and it needn't be returned. Thus the floodgates were opened; ten pounds here, twenty pounds there, none of which ever found its way back into the Bell's coffers.

George also knew that the pub itself was actually doing well. It just so happened that its landlord was pissing away the profits up the proverbial wall of whichever bookmaker he didn't owe money to ... which wasn't many. Angus had a habit that was spiralling out of control and the only way he could deal with it was to drink or to ask for another hand-out, both of which he did in excess. George had had enough.

"It's a nice party George," Angus commented as he tried to focus on his host.

"How much this time?" George asked directly.

Angus frowned. "What do ye mean? Ah jus' ...?"

"How much Angus?" George cut in, not wanting to play games with this fool. Angus remained silent for a moment and then snorted a laugh, pointing towards George with an unsteady, glass holding hand.

"Ye know me too well son!" he slurred, and then hiccupped. "Ah don't like to ask but ... "

"How much?" George cut in again, losing what little patience he had left.

Angus looked towards the house to make sure nobody was close by and then turned back to George. "Well, forty if ye can manage it son?" he replied, trying to look and sound as humble as he could. But his eyes suddenly lit up with greedy excitement when George opened his wallet and revealed its contents. "Fifty, tops!" He quickly added, hoping that George would extend his benevolence to the latter amount. George counted out one hundred pounds then held it out towards his father-in-law. Angus couldn't believe his luck. "That's very generous Son!" he exclaimed as he reached out to take the money. "An Ah'll pay ye back jus' as ..."

George suddenly withdrew the cash from Angus's reach and scowled at him. "Let this be the last time ye ever ask me or Lilly for money, do ye understand Angus?" he said sharply. Angus frowned and almost wanted to protest. After all, he was family and what were a few pounds here and there between families? But then he saw the look in George's eyes, a look he had seen before and remembered all too well. He quickly nodded his understanding. George suddenly moved a lot closer making Angus flinch slightly. "Ah want tae be sure that ye are clear on this Angus?" George continued, with a tone of menace. "'Cause if Ah ever hear that ye huv asked Lilly for so much as one more penny tae take a piss with, ye'll huv me tae deal with!" Angus swallowed hard. George continued to stare. The silence was deafening. When George held out the cash for a second time, Angus took it without hesitation, hurriedly stuffing the wad of notes into his pocket before George had time to change his mind.

George shook his head and began to walk away, suddenly stopping just beyond Angus. "An' one more thing," he started.

Angus maintained the same false expression of humility on his perspiring face as George leant in towards him. "Name it," he offered, trying to force an accommodating smile.

George could smell the stale odour of alcohol-infused sweat on his father-in-law that for some reason, infuriated him more. He narrowed his eyes before growling his final demand at the pathetic man before him. "Don't ever call me *son* again!"

George held Angus in his stare for a moment longer making sure his words had been understood. When Angus shrugged then nodded, George walked back towards the house, somehow knowing that this wouldn't be the end of the matter.

Angus began to smirk as he watched George disappear into the house ... he was already planning how he could continue to tap into his daughter's generosity without George finding out.

Over the few months that followed Lilly's birthday, George noticed a considerable change in her personality. It was as though her otherwise chirpy and positive attitude was being physically and mentally sapped from her body as she became extremely short tempered, quiet, depressed and highly emotional. Margaret had assured George that it was all part and parcel of being pregnant but George felt ... knew ... there was definitely something more to it.

On the 3rd August 1970, George came home to find Lilly sitting on the floor, crying uncontrollably. It took George the best part of thirty minutes to comfort and reassure his wife before she could actually speak to him with any real comprehensibility. Only then did George discover the real reason behind Lilly's upset. He learned that, despite the stern warning, Angus had continued to feed off Lilly's good nature by asking her for more hand-outs. And not only had the amounts increased, but so had the frequency in which they were being asked for. Unacceptable in itself, but the explanation as to why the money was needed had, in George's mind, put Angus amongst a breed of parasites that were in a league of their own ... and he was livid.

###

Angus McBride

23

The life of Angus McBride was never destined to be straightforward. The only child of Jacob and Ann McBride, (original licensee's of The Jolly Piper public house) his every need was catered for and there was no doubt that this would continue right up until the eventual death of his doting parents. But the smothering love from his mother (brought about as a result of the premature death of her first child) and the lack of discipline from his father caused Angus to become spoilt and assume ... or rather expect ... that everybody else would treat him exactly the same.

When his parents were tragically killed in a freak boating accident in 1922 (their vessel being struck by a random sea mine left over from World War One) Angus found it to be a great inconvenience. Yes, he grieved a while and yes, it perturbed him that the only thing that could be found of his parents was his father's old binocular's case. But what was more daunting to Angus is that he'd suddenly been left a thriving pub that he had no idea how to run. And why should he? After all, he'd never had to think or do anything for himself in his entire eighteen years of living.

Angus decided that the best way to keep the order of things on an even keel was to find himself a wife. And that's just what he did. Unfortunately for Angus, his bride turned out to be lazy and inattentive yet more than willing to help herself to the spoils of the pub's profits whenever she needed something new ... which was quite often. The latter trait, Angus could probably have lived with but not having clean clothes or a proper meal on the table at the appropriate times was just too much to cope with. Hence, Mrs McBride number one was unceremoniously dismissed just under a year later ... as indeed was Mrs McBride number two eighteen months after that.

Mrs McBride number three ... Margaret ... turned out to be a whole new kettle of fish. Though attentive, house proud and able to manage the pub when needed, she didn't suffer fools gladly and soon had Angus transformed from a grown up spoilt child into a decent kind of husband who learnt that giving was actually a two way street ... a concept that he would have found unimaginable at one stage in his life.

Angus developed a new and uncharacteristic feeling towards Margaret that he concluded was called *being in love* and what's more, he liked it. And when Margaret announced that she was expecting their child, his eyes and heart opened to a whole new world of excitement and happiness. He wondered why Margaret didn't seem as overjoyed as he, but she managed to allay his suspicions by blaming it on the trepidation of their new beginnings.

"Och, we'll be fine Margaret," he had assured her. "Ah couldnae huv wished for anything more!" Margaret smiled the best she could. "And ye know what?" he added holding her face in his hands. "Ye'll make a great mum!" He smiled, kissed her on the forehead and then held her close.

In that moment, Margaret was thankful that Angus couldn't read her mind. She was also thankful that he was useless with dates, otherwise he might have realised that he was away at some Landlord's convention when the child was actually conceived.

Angus liked a *flutter*. After all, which man didn't like the occasional bet or two on the horses, the dogs or the odd bare-knuckle fight ... which is how he first met Isaac incidentally. But as much as Isaac was a *sure bet* for Angus at the time, things didn't go quite as smoothly for him when Isaac gave up the fighting and returned to fishing. That's when the small seed of addiction began to grow and rear its ugly head. You see, whilst Angus was initially breaking even with a win here and a loss there, he was always under the false illusion that the big pay-out was just around the corner, hence, his wagers began to increase ... negligible at first but increases none the less.

As time went by, Angus would bet on virtually anything the bookmaker's would give him odds on. He even placed a bet of five pounds on the sex of his unborn child once. The return, if he won, wouldn't have been day changing let alone life changing but nevertheless Angus knew he was onto a winner. He knew by the shape of his wife during her pregnancy, both his and her genetic make-up and the tried and tested method of instinct, that this small, *dead cert* bet, would turn the tide of fortune in his favour and lead to bigger and better things in the future. It would definitely be a boy and make no mistake ... here Bookie, take my cash!

When Lilly was born, Angus was far from disappointed. Yes, he'd lost a bet but had gained what he thought to be the most beautiful thing in the whole world. He even managed to curb his passion for anything with a starting price as he concentrated on bringing his daughter up. Angus took his new responsibility very seriously, knowing that he would need to watch every penny so that Lilly could have the best of everything, whether it be toys, clothes or even the choice of education. "Good schools are no' cheap Margaret," he had said to his wife on numerous occasions. "And unless ye want our daughter to grow up with oot a brain in her head, then private tuition is the only answer!"

But as the years passed, Angus's working day became longer and harder as he fought to keep up with the fees for

Lilly's education. And although he didn't resent the reason behind his need to work hard, it brought about an immense amount of stress that led him to become both irritable and unapproachable. It also led him to drink more alcohol with the occasional *pick me up* becoming a regular *keep me up*. Margaret had tried to speak to him about it but when she was met with a barrage of abuse and told to stop interfering, she never mentioned it again. In fact, from that particular day onwards, Margaret mentioned very little to Angus turning instead to Isaac whenever she needed a confidant and advisory council. He was so calm and logical and always spoke with a tone that lifted Margaret's spirits. But of course, like so many other things in her life, there was a downside to this growing dependency on Isaac's moral support ... each time she listened to his words, she had no choice but to mentally kick herself and silently confess to making the wrong choice of husband.

Angus could pinpoint the exact time when his passion (not addiction) for gambling came home to roost. It was the day following the announcement by Lilly that she planned to marry that no hoper, George Bell. He despised the man. Not just because he had somehow wormed his way into her life but also because he had managed to deflect her attention away from him, her own father. But Angus wasn't fooled by Bell's gentle ways and sickening show of affection towards Lilly, no sir, not like Margaret and Isaac had been ... what sort of a mother and godfather falls for that sort of nonsense anyway? He knew that George saw a free meal ticket in Lilly and bet that it wouldn't be long until his daughter realised that too and left him. But it was another bet that Angus stood to lose.

And so, with the shift of his daughter's affections to another man and a seemingly dis-interested and inattentive wife, Angus decided that the bookmakers would offer him all the excitement he needed and make him a few pounds in the process. But his rekindled hobby would yield neither excitement nor monetary gain and after a few large losses that were all but impossible to cover, Angus was forced onto the ropes. And as each of the more reputable Turf Accountants closed their doors on Angus (writing off his debts as a lost cause), the less forgiving and far from legal establishments welcomed him with open arms ... and there lay his downfall.

For Angus, the only saving grace in his dark world of gambling, was that the people in his community loved to drink and this made The Jolly Piper accounts show some very healthy profits ... profits that Angus used on several occasions to ward off many threatened visits from debt collectors. If Margaret ever asked where the profits were actually ending up, he would always assure her that they were being used for long-term investments. "Our retirement nest egg!" he would proclaim, although Margaret was never wholly convinced. And if the rumours and the concerns from Isaac were anything to go by, not only was there no egg but the nest hadn't even begun to be constructed.

Things took a turn for the worst when Margaret, spurred on by an impromptu visit from an unsavoury *acquaintance* of her husband, confronted Angus face to face. Finding himself backed into a corner, Angus broke down and confessed all ... well, almost all ... admitting that he had been a fool and weak whilst pleading for forgiveness. To his surprise, Margaret did forgive him but insisted on two conditions. "Name them," he had replied with exaggerated remorse.

"Firstly, you find help for your gambling and your drinking addictions!" she said sternly.

Angus had agreed whole-heartedly, stating that it was a small price to pay whilst secretly thinking, *'we'll see!'*

"And secondly," she continued, without breaking her stare. "Ye give me full control over the finances of the pub. And Ah mean *full* control!"

Angus frowned. "But how am Ah ..." he started.

"Those are my conditions Angus," Margaret cut in. "If ye no agree, then Ah will leave ye and ye can sort out your own mess. It's your choice!"

Angus was in a corner. He didn't want his monetary lifeline being scrutinised and no doubt stopped but neither did he want to lose his wife. He thought about asking for some time to consider the proposal but realised that that would be all the incentive Margaret needed to leave him there and then. Reluctantly, he had agreed, managing to keep the same expression of remorse and gratitude on his face as he did so.

Angus needed to rethink his plan as all avenues of credit were closed in favour of cash only transactions and the debt collectors (of which Margaret knew only half of) didn't take cheques ... they would however, add a little interest to the outstanding debts and physically advise him whenever he missed a payment if he so required? Without access to the pub's funds, Angus found himself on a very steep and very slippery downward slope. He was heading for one of two things; either a sure-fire divorce (if Margaret ever found out that he wasn't on the books of any gambling councillor) or worse still, a long time in hospital for services rendered. The alcohol helped but he could only stay drunk for some of the time!

And then, as if a strange and twisted God was looking down on him with misguided compassion, Isaac died leaving the majority of his wealth to Lilly ... lifeline restored, thank you O Heavenly Father!!

But Angus, disguising his greed as a genuine request for help, became excessive in the number of times he would ask his daughter for cash with each occasion seeing an increase in the amount asked for. In fact, in the three months that followed the inheritance of Isaac's estate, Lilly saw more of her father's outstretched wanton hand than she did her own husband. Although she initially remained silent about helping

---

146

her father out, she decided, a week before her birthday, that the time had come to tell George everything ... just after the point where her father's requests began to sound very much like demands.

###

4th August 1970 ... Angus woke up in the same position that he had fallen asleep in the night before and cursed. The armchair had not only irritated his lower back problem but also served to remind him why he had slept on it in the first place. He called out for his wife but the absence of a reply told him that he was alone. He'd not seen the note that Margaret had left and so had no idea where his wife actually was. Truth was, it didn't really matter to him at that moment in time. In fact, she and that daughter of hers could go to Hell and back for all he cared ... they meant nothing to him anymore, nobody did!

He reached for the whisky bottle sitting on the table next to him and emptied the final dregs into his mouth. He wasn't drunk just yet but he certainly intended to be. He got up from the chair with a pained grunt, made his way into the cellar and selected another bottle of twelve-year-old single malt from the pub's rapidly depleting stock. "There's no need for a glass thank you landlord!" he muttered to himself as he removed the top and gulped a large shot straight from the bottle. Pulling it away from his mouth with a contented sigh, he studied the label for a moment and then lifted the bottle slightly in a gesture of silent homage to the distillers of Glenmorangie. "Thank you Landlord," he said to the half lit emptiness of the cellar. "Ah will now retire to ma lounge tae enjoy this liquid nectar in peace!"

A few minutes later, Angus was back in his armchair holding the bottle of whisky against his chest. The small table sitting next to him was now considered to be an inappropriate resting place for the bottle as that would mean having to reach out for it every time he needed to take a drink and what a waste of energy that would be. Plus, he had no intention of putting the bottle down until it had been drained of all its contents anyway, so what was the point? And as if to confirm this, Angus took another large gulp.

As his mind began to dwell on past events, he felt himself becoming angry. Not with himself but at the fact that Lilly had gone and told that fool husband of hers all about the money she had leant him ... as if it was his business anyway! If she hadn't told him, then maybe none of this current mess would have come about in the first place. He took another mouthful of whisky. But then he chuckled slightly as he recalled how that same fool husband had warned him against asking for any more money whilst at the same time handing him a most welcome one hundred pounds in cash. What an idiot! He took another mouthful of whisky. And then another. And anyway, did he not realise that blood was thicker than water? "Ha!" he suddenly scoffed out loud, as thoughts of the previous evenings argument with his daughter came flooding back. "Blood thicker than water? ... what a joke ... no' even ma blood are ye missy?" He remained silent again, his red-eyed stare fixed on nothing in particular. When the first tear ran down his cheek, he quickly wiped it away and took another mouthful of whisky in the hope that it would stop his mind from thinking back ... it didn't.

###

A couple of months after the warning and subsequent cash injection from George, Angus was back on his arse, struggling to pay his gambling debts. Margaret already had full control of the pub's cash flow and with the doorway to Lilly's inheritance firmly closed, Angus found his future looking pretty grim ... again! And then, like a Perry line to a drowning man, an opportunity presented itself to Angus that he wasted little time taking advantage of, manipulating the details to suit his purpose.

When Margaret became unwell with a strong viral infection, she ended up being confined to her bed for a number of weeks. Though ultimately not life threatening, the Doctor had advised that she rest completely and have as little contact with others as possible, especially Lilly, given that she was pregnant ... bingo! Angus began to formulate a plan. Once he had disguised the true facts about Margaret's illness and convinced his daughter not to see her for a while, the time came to put the finishing touches of that plan into action.

"How is she today? Lilly had asked during one of her visits.

And ... Action!

Angus bowed his head and remained silent. Lilly frowned anxiously. "Dad? What is it? What's wrong?" she pressed.

After a moment longer of silence, Angus looked up and set about telling his daughter how Margaret's condition was getting worse and that the Doctor had told him that without certain tablets and medicines, her condition would deteriorate rapidly. But they were expensive as the NHS wouldn't subsidise them and he didn't know how he would be able to afford them, what with the pub not doing so well and all. And he was scared of losing her because of his failings and had no idea what to do next? "Oh Lilly!" he finished, even managing to shed a little tear as he told her the devastating news!

"Oh Dad," Lilly had said, putting her arms around him. "Why didn't you say something sooner, instead of worrying like this? Ah can pay for what she needs, you should know that? You only needed to ask!"

Angus looked at her through his watery eyes. "And what sort of a husband would that make me, that Ah cannae even look after ma own wife without asking for charity? Ah'm no' fit tae be ...!" He broke off, put his head in his hands and wept. Perfect. A performance that even Gielgud would aspire to deliver.

"It's not charity," Lilly insisted, trying to comfort Angus. "And even if it means using all my money to get mum better again, then that's what Ah'll do!"

With his face still hidden in the palm of his hands, Angus allowed himself to smile. *'Oh the sweetness of loyalty served with a small helping of innocent naivety!'* he thought.

Angus downed another mouthful of whisky shaking his head at his own stupidity. Did he really believe that Lilly wouldn't realise his ploy as soon as her mother was up and about again and clearly not as ill as he had made out? Maybe, maybe not. But he had intended to cross that bridge when he came to it. Trouble was, when the time to cross that particular bridge came about, Lilly just wouldn't listen to anything he had to say. Maybe she should have just been happy with the fact that her mother was ok, he thought, rather than attack him for a slight exaggeration of the truth? And he was going to pay all the money back anyway ... eventually. But she couldn't see that, could she? And who was she to raise her voice to him, her own father? ...

"Ha, my own father!" she had spat. "Ah can assure you that you're no father of mine!" Angus tried to get up from his armchair to protest, but fell right back into it. She took a step forward, picked up the half empty bottle of whisky sitting on the small table next to him, and gave him a look of utter contempt. "But Ah guess you're too drunk, too stupid and too busy conning me out of the money *he* left me to realise who my real father is! ... aren't you Angus?"

Angus frowned. "What the hell does that mean?" he hissed.

"Exactly what Ah said!" Lilly replied. "You're not my father, Isaac was!"

"What? ... You're a bloody liar!" Angus shouted. "Why would ye say that?"

"Because it's true!" Lilly shouted back. "And there is only one liar in this room, Angus!" Lilly leant in towards him. "You disgust me!" she whispered. Angus looked at her open-mouthed, speechless. Lilly studied him for a moment, thinking just how pathetic he looked at that moment. He reminded her of a dog that had been scolded. She should have walked away there and then leaving him with nothing more than a vision of her utter disdain in his mind. But she couldn't. She was better than that. She sighed and crouched down in front of Angus, her expression mellowing slightly.

Angus saw a glimmer of hope, a small possibility that forgiveness could be on the horizon and he intended to grab it with both hands. She'd obviously said what she'd said just to try and hurt him and for a moment, it had worked. He'd let her have that one, given his own recent actions. But she wasn't the cruel or vindictive type he thought and she wouldn't just walk away from him. She was better than that. He smiled at her, hopefully.

"Oh Angus," she sighed again, gently placing her hand on the top of his. "Why couldn't you have ... ?"

"Ah know, Ah know!" he interjected. "Ah should huv told ye and Ah'm sorry fae what Ah did! Can ye ever ..."

"No no, you misunderstand!" Lilly cut in quietly, patting his hand as she spoke. Angus frowned, a little confused. "What Ah was going to say," Lilly continued, now smiling slightly. "Is why, if there is a fair and just God looking down on us all, couldn't you have died instead of Isaac?" Angus's jaw dropped open. "It's just not right!" Lilly glared at Angus allowing her final words to take hold as he realised just how much she despised him ... Now she could walk away!

Angus took yet another large swig from the rapidly emptying whisky bottle, still trying to blot out the memory of the day before. It wasn't working.

He had watched Lilly walk out of the front door, slamming it behind her as she left leaving a broken man in her wake. He would never have imagined her to be so cutting and nasty towards him but knew, in all honesty, that there was only one person to blame ... himself! But there again, hadn't she lied to him and worse still, had Margaret not led him a merry dance for all these years. *'Couple of scheming bitches!'* he thought as he drank some more. "So bloody self righteous aren't ye?" he accused the absent before drinking some more. "Up there on your high horses!" he continued. "Who are ye to judge me?"

He had seen how much Lilly had hated him and it hurt. He had seen how she had walked out of his house without even glancing back; so cold and void of love. What he had not seen is how Lilly had broken down in tears outside his front door and then clutched her stomach as a gripping pain shot through her.

And now, just over twelve hours later, he was sitting in his lounge on the brink of total inebriation, feeling an incredible loneliness that he had never felt before. He looked around the room in a bid to focus his mind on something else and suddenly spotted an envelope left on the mantle piece. He squinted, trying to see the words written on the front but realised that he would have to get up from his chair if he wanted any chance of reading it. He placed the whisky bottle onto the table beside him and grunted again as he pushed himself slowly out of the chair. He had taken only a few steps towards the envelope, when the front door of his home was suddenly thrown open, drenching him and the room in bright sunlight. He turned towards the door, holding his hand up to shield his eyes against the blinding glare but had no problem in recognising the person who had dared to enter his domain without an invite. "O aye? ... An' what the fuck d' ye want?" were the only words said.

24

3rd August 1970. George stood up and made his way to the door. "Where are you going?" Lilly asked. She looked totally drained of colour except for the redness of her eyes that were stinging from the amount of tears that she had shed that evening.

"Ah need tae huv a wee word with Angus!" George replied, though the tone of his voice suggested it was not going to be a friendly word.

"No George, please!" Lilly pleaded. "He's not worth it and Ah ... ow!"

George watched his wife grimace with pain, holding her stomach. "What is it Lilly? Are ye ok?" He rushed over to her side and put an arm around her. "Is it the baby?"

"It's just a twinge," she lied. "Nothing to worry about!" She smiled at George who was far too concerned to smile back.

"How long huv ye been huving them?" he asked. "Shall Ah get the Doctor?"

"Ah'm fine George, really. You could get me a glass of water though, please!"

George leapt to his feet and disappeared into the kitchen just as another shooting pain hit Lilly's stomach. More painful and longer than any she had experienced, Lilly knew that something wasn't right.

George opened the tap and let the water run whilst he went to find a glass. He looked in the cupboard where they were normally stored but found none. After a couple more hasty yet unsuccessful searches in other cupboards he decided that Lilly had no doubt had another clear out and decided to change everything about. "Lilly!" he shouted. "Where huv ye put the glasses this time?" He stopped mid-search when he got no reply and frowned. "Lilly?" he called again, now walking back into the lounge. He found Lilly sat upright on the edge of her seat, looking towards her lap with panic on her face. "Lilly, what is it?" he asked softly as he moved towards her. When he knelt down beside his wife, she turned to him with quivering lips and tried to speak. Nothing would come out. As tears over spilled from her eyes, she looked back towards her lap causing George to instinctively follow suit. "Oh sweet Jesus!" he gasped.

Lilly had no idea that George had run off to get help, nor was she aware when he returned with the doctor less than five minutes later. In the numbness of shock, Lilly had not moved an inch ... except to brush her hand, gently yet constantly, against the cloth of her blood sodden skirt.

George anxiously paced the landing outside the closed door of his bedroom listening to the pained screams coming from within. Never in all his life had he felt so useless, knowing that at this point, he could nothing to help his wife.

When he had returned to the house with the doctor an hour earlier, he was immediately instructed to carry Lilly up to their bedroom, call the midwife and provide some boiling water and clean towels ... there was no time to get Lilly to a hospital, the doctor had informed him, as it would appear that the baby was wanting to come out a lot sooner than expected. George quickly did as he was told whilst all the time cursing himself for his own incredible stupidity. For in the panic of the situation, he had completely forgotten that they'd recently had a telephone installed and could have used it to get the doctor to attend a lot faster.

Once George had informed the midwife and gotten the doctor all that he required, he telephoned Lilly's mum. Margaret had barely finished speaking to George when she had written a small note to her sleeping husband, collected what she needed and was out of the front door making her way to be with her daughter. She would update Angus later with any news, if he was sober ... or if she could be bothered speaking to him at all!

###

Margaret McBride

25

When Margaret accepted Angus's proposal of marriage, she was sure of only two things. The first was that she had no intention of being treated like Mrs McBride one or two and the second, she had no real idea why she had said yes in the first place. Maybe it was a knee jerk reaction, influenced by the sad look of expectant rejection on Angus's face the day he popped the question. Or maybe it was to get back at the one person she truly loved but who, at that time, seemed to treat the idea of monogamy as a sin rather than a virtue.

And so, despite her many reservations, the marriage to Angus went ahead and she vowed to be the best wife a woman could be. In the eyes of the public, she carried this off with convincing style and in time, actually discovered a fondness for Angus that she never thought she would have. But there was no confusing this feeling with actually *being* in love, as that emotion had been saved and filed under the heading of the man for whom it was originally intended ... Isaac Andrews!

Margaret knew that her own mother had been unfaithful and had witnessed the unpleasant consequences that the discovery of her infidelity had brought. As a result, she made a promise to herself never to follow the example of her mother but remain true to her own spouse whenever the time came for her to be a wife. So, when she found herself being tempted into an affair by Isaac, she initially stood by those beliefs, dismissing his many advances with the frequently used phrase; "You had your chance Isaac Andrews!"

But life has a way of throwing in anomalies that constantly alter the way we think and feel and with the diminishing attention from Angus she found herself being drawn more and more onto the same path as her mother. In the end, she resigned herself to the fact that resistance was futile and the fight to maintain her morals soon became a battle to ease her guilt.

However, when she found out that she was pregnant with Isaac's child, the panic shook her back into reality, falsely re-kindling her belief that marriage was for life, for better or for worse. Her time with Isaac, as warm and as loving as it had been, needed to come to an end. And though her decision wasn't helped by Isaac's desire to run away and start a new life together, her mind was made up. Whatever failings Angus had as a husband, she explained to Isaac, he didn't deserve to be made a laughing stock of through her selfish act. Tempted as she was with Isaac's pleas and promises of a better future with him, she convinced herself that they were just shallow words; words which Isaac would undoubtedly have regretted in later life. It was painfully ironic that the only person with later regrets was Margaret herself.

Much to Margaret's surprise, Angus became a devoted father and husband, blissfully unaware that Lilly wasn't his. He didn't even question her choice of godfather that she had suggested with an unwarranted amount of enthusiasm. She quickly checked herself. "He's not ideal, Ah know," she added trying to disguise her emotions. "But you huv known Isaac a long time and our baby does need a godparent Ah suppose!" Angus had not only agreed but insisted on asking Isaac himself thus confirming, to Margaret's relief, that her husband remained ignorant of the truth.

But in the years that followed Lilly's birth, Margaret saw a decline in two things; the pub's profits and Angus's devotion to her or his daughter, the latter seemingly becoming worse once a certain George Bell had come onto the scene. Was it jealousy, that Lilly now gave George more attention than her father? Was it anger, borne from an unfounded belief that Lilly was ungrateful for the sacrifices that had been made to afford her a good education? Or was it simply that Angus no longer cared for either of them? Though Margaret pondered on the many possibilities, she wouldn't have come close to knowing the actual reason for the change in his personality, until the day that somebody knocked on her front door.

"Can Ah help ye?" she had asked, frowning at the stranger now standing before her. Her immediate and bizarre train of thought was that men like this only existed in gangster films shown at the cinema, not outside her home. His course tone brought her quickly back to reality.

"Ah'd like a wee word with Angus!" the man replied without any hint of pleasantry in his voice.

"Can Ah ask what it's about?" she quizzed, still frowning. The man sighed and took a step forward, peering over Margaret's shoulder into the house as if he was looking for the man he had come to see. Margaret instinctively shifted her body to block the man's progression but given that he was about six foot six inches tall and equally as wide, she knew that if he'd wanted to gain entry, then that's exactly what he would have done. She began to worry. "He's not here," she lied, trying to speak without her voice shaking. "But Ah can give him a message if ye just ...!"

"That won't be necessary," he interrupted, starring intently at Margaret with a slight, yet dis-comforting smile. He eventually broke his stare and peered back into the house.

"Ah will catch up with him, eventually!" he added, raising his voice slightly as though wanting to project his words to whomever else might be listening. He stepped back and looked again at Margaret with that same cold smile. She shivered. "Until next time then, Mrs McBride!" he said with a slight air of menace in his voice, before he turned and walked away. Margaret stood frozen to the spot, wanting to close the door but unable to. The unexpected voice behind her, made her jump and look round.

"Close the bloody door woman," Angus whispered, skulking behind his armchair.

Margaret turned back around and felt her stomach flip as she saw that the stranger had stopped mid-way along the garden path and was now looking directly at her. *'Oh my God, he heard Angus!'* she thought with dread. She didn't know this man, had no idea what he wanted Angus for and couldn't explain why she felt so intimidated by him ... she just did! And now she had no doubt that he was about to force his way into her home, inflict some form of harm on Angus (and possibly her) and there was absolutely nothing she could do or say to stop it. She waited for the inevitable to happen as the man continued to stare. And then, with precise purpose, he reached slowly into the inside pocket of his jacket. Fear gripped Margaret.

"Has he gone?" Angus whispered from behind.

'He's got a gun!' she wanted to scream but neither words nor sound would come out of her dry, open mouth.

"Margaret ... has he gone?" Angus repeated anxiously.

'Oh Jesus!' Margaret thought, visibly shaking as she watched the man pulling the firearm from his pocket. *'We're going to die!'* When she saw that the weapon was actually a packet of Capstan full strength, she almost collapsed with relief.

The man lit a cigarette, inhaled deeply and then exhaled the blue tinged smoke high into the air above his head. He then looked back at Margaret with the same unnerving smile. "Beautiful day Mrs McBride," he remarked casually. "Would ye no' agree?"

Margaret stood aghast only just managing to nod her head slowly. He took another drag of the cigarette, held Margaret in his stare for a moment longer and then left. Only when the stranger had walked beyond the garden gate was Margaret able to summon enough strength to close her front door, falling to her knees behind it as she sobbed.

That was the day that Margaret had discovered exactly what Angus had been up to and how his gambling and drinking addictions were almost out of control. It was also the day that she realised something very important ... that trust was no longer an emotion she could ever offer Angus again.

When Isaac passed away, Margaret was gripped by an overwhelming sorrow. Not just because the one man she had ever really loved had gone but also because Lilly, his daughter, had never got to hear the truth about who he was. Margaret had wanted to tell her for years (as did Isaac) but, as is always the case with such delicate matters, she was waiting for the right time. The trouble with hiding behind that particular philosophy though, is that the *right time* never seemed to present itself and now ... well now, it was just too late! Maybe it was for the best, she thought, let sleeping dogs lie and all that! And so, rightly or wrongly, she had decided that leaving Lilly with just the memories of a loving *godfather* would probably be the best course of action. The discovery and subsequent reading of Isaac's last will and testament soon put paid to that idea!

When Lilly visited her mother the day following the reading, Margaret listened to all that had been revealed by Mr Patterson and expected a barrage of accusations and hurtful comments to follow. To her utter surprise Lilly not only remained extremely calm, but remarkably, forgave her mother's past indiscretion unconditionally. "Ah can see how you were attracted to him," she had said. "He could charm the birds out of the trees, that one!"

Mother and her daughter spent the rest of that morning talking about Isaac ... laughing, crying ... but mostly, regretting what hadn't been said or done in the time that he was alive. For Margaret, the weight from years of a troubled conscience had finally been lifted from her shoulders and she doubted that she could ever feel closer to Lilly than she did at that point. That was until Lilly revealed that she was pregnant.

Margaret was overjoyed with the news that she was at last, going to become a grandmother. Yet, the more Lilly blossomed, the more Margaret became the world's greatest worrier. This worry, together with keeping an eye on the Pub and an even bigger eye on her inattentive husband, were probable contributors to her becoming run down and then contracting a viral infection. It completely wiped her out and when she was confined to her bed with instructions not to have too much contact with her pregnant daughter, she couldn't think of a worse situation. She couldn't fuss over Lilly (her yin) but neither could she keep a check on Angus (her yang).

Only when she had recovered did she get to hear how Angus had actually used his temporary free reign and it surpassed even Margaret's thoughts on what he was capable of. Both embarrassed and disgusted by his behaviour, harsh and bitter words together with a firm promise of divorce were soon delivered to Angus. There would be no forgiveness this time round and he could forget any idea of sleeping in their bed for the foreseeable future!

But none of that really mattered anymore. Not the pub, not Angus's deceit or addictions, none of it. What did matter, was the telephone call that Margaret had received from George later that evening. A telephone call that had led her to be sitting in Lilly's bedroom now, holding the hand of her suffering daughter.

###

26

George continued to pace the floor outside his bedroom door, grimacing at every pained cry that came from within, hopeful with every moment of silence. He had never been much of a religious man before but he'd lost count the number of times he had asked God for some form of divine intervention in the past nine hours. He felt helpless and had to stop himself, on more than one occasion, from storming into the room and demanding that he be given something, anything, to do.

During one of the rare interludes of prolonged silence, Margaret came out of the room forcing a smile onto her tired and worried face. She gave George a hug and assured him that everything would be ok. "She may be weak," Margaret said. "But she won't give up until that child of yours makes an appearance!" George tried to smile back but enthusiasm and expectant joy had been replaced by uncertainty and concern, causing his face to remain in a contorted frown.

"Tell her Ah love her Margaret, please?" George asked sadly.

"Ah think you can tell her yourself!" a voice suddenly announced from behind them. They both looked round and saw the doctor standing by the bedroom door. George gasped when he saw the amount of blood of the doctor's hands. Margaret went back into the room but as George started to follow, the doctor gently took a hold of his arm, stopping him from entering. George, still frowning, looked down at the doctor's hand grasping his elbow and then quickly back to the doctor himself, confused.

"Can Ah huv a wee word before ye go in George?" the doctor said with a sombre tone.

George panicked. "She's going tae be all right isn't she?" he gulped, trying not to think about the dried blood on the doctor's hands. The doctor sighed yet kept a neutral expression on his face making it impossible for George to second-guess what was on his mind.

"Ah'm no' going tae lie tae ye George," he said quietly whilst looking George straight in the eye. "She's lost a lot of blood and she is very weak. And Ah cannae risk getting her tae a hospital in her current state ... " he trailed off as though considering what he needed to say next and looked awkwardly down towards the floor.

"What is it'?" George probed. "Doctor?" he quickly added when the response wasn't immediate.

"Ah think she might huv tae lose the baby George!" the doctor replied, looking back up at him. George's lips began to quiver. "Ah know it's a terrible thing tae hear George," he quickly continued. "But if she has this baby, well Ah ... " he paused.

"What?" George asked with a trembling voice.

The doctor sighed again. "The truth is George, if she has the baby, Ah'm might not be able to save either of them ... !"

"No, no, nooo!" George suddenly cried out, throwing his hands up to his head whilst turning away.

"Ah'm so terribly sorry George, fae the both of ye!" the doctor continued, sympathetically. "But Ah cannae ..."

The doctor stopped mid sentence as a loud cry of pain suddenly came from the bedroom causing both him and George to swing around.

"Doctor. Please. Come Quickly!" the voice of the midwife called out with great urgency.

"Stay here George!" he instructed sternly as he ran back into the bedroom and slammed the door behind him. For a short while, George stood completely still, rooted to the spot as he glared at the closed door that was stopping him from being with his wife. He then started to cry. Fearing that hope was slowly but surely slipping away, he fell to his knees, put his clasped, trembling hands up towards his mouth and began to pray.

An hour later, the doctor emerged from the bedroom once more, his head bowed low. George realised, well before he had seen the doctor's tearful eyes, that something had gone terribly wrong. He raced past the doctor and into the bedroom not even registering the midwife who had started to say something to him. He stopped and stared at his wife lay motionless on the bed, his initial thoughts conveying how strangely peaceful she now looked. And then it hit him. He glanced at Margaret sat by Lilly's side, sobbing yet speaking softly to her as she moved strands of sodden hair from her daughter's face.

George moved slowly towards his wife, leant down and kissed her gently on the forehead. "Ah love ye Mrs Bell!" he said, tenderly. He wiped away his own tears that had fallen on Lilly's cheek and then kissed her on the lips. Moving his mouth to Lilly's ear he whispered. "Ah'll miss ye so much!"

A few moments later George pulled away, his immediate grief temporarily replaced by anger. As he wiped his eyes and looked down at Lilly, he tried to justify the reasons why his wife lay dead and yet that bastard Angus still lived. After all, was it not him who had been the sole contributor to Lilly's upset and stress that had now resulted in her death? He had abused his position as husband and father on so many occasions with no regard whatsoever for the hurt or upset he may have caused. It seemed so unfair that God, in his infinite wisdom, chose to take his loving and caring wife rather than a worthless man who was drinking himself into an early grave anyway ... somebody needed to redress the balance.

George got up and ran out the room neither hearing nor caring what the doctor, the midwife and Margaret were beginning to say.

He didn't stop running until he had reached the front door of Angus's house and only then to kick it open.

He immediately saw Angus stood in the lounge and felt a new and incredible surge of wrath that completely dwarfed his initial anger.

"O aye? ... An' what the fuck d' ye want?" Angus quizzed in a drunken slur.

It was all the excuse that George needed.

27

I looked at George, unable ... no ... not wanting to speak. What could I have said that would have made the slightest bit of difference to the way this man was probably feeling right now as he recounted this terrible and heart rendering episode of his life.

"Ye ok son?" George suddenly asked, breaking away from the clutches of his history. I felt a little embarrassed when I realised he had seen a tear fall from my eye and I quietly blamed its appearance on the curse of hay fever.

George nodded and gave me an understanding smile. "Can be a nightmare, Ah'm sure!" he said supportively. "Though Ah'm sure Ah read somewhere that Bicarbonate of Soda helps. Would ye like some?" he added with an impish smile. I'm sure we both knew the answer to that one!

"Can I ask you something George?" I said after a small pause.

"Well, nothing's stopped ye so far!" he replied with the same smile.

I smiled back though didn't immediately ask the question I wanted to ask. I pondered on it a moment wondering if it might have been a little inappropriate, especially as it was only to satisfy my morbid curiosity. But after all he had put Lilly and Margaret through, I really wanted to know. "What did you do to Angus?" I asked. For some reason, the very second I had put the question to him, I made an unconscious fist with my hand and twitched my arm as though I was about to throw a punch. It wasn't an outwardly obvious movement by any means but certainly not one that George missed as he quickly glanced down and raised his eyebrows.

"Ah did something that was rash and hot headed ... and it's the reason, Ah suppose, that Ah'm livin' like Ah am now!"

I frowned, wondering what it was he'd done that was so bad. I wasn't left wondering for long.

George lunged at Angus landing a right hook that would have put Mohammed Ali on the seat of his pants. Angus, too slow and too drunk to offer any kind of defensive stance, took the full blow to the left side of his face, seemingly lifting off the ground as the fist made impact. As if in slow motion, Angus collapsed sideways, falling towards the fireplace with awkward grace. George gasped in a moment of stark realisation as he saw what Angus, or rather his head, was going to make contact with. Whether it was panic or just a feeling of regret, George made a grab at the falling man's arm but it was too late. And then there was a sickening thud as Angus's head struck the cast iron grate and immediately opened up, allowing a steady stream of blood to flow out and form its own macabre pool on the floor beside him.

George looked on in horror. He quickly knelt down beside Angus and called his name, gently shaking him in a bid to bring him round. But the man didn't stir ... it didn't even look like he was breathing.

In a moment of dread, George feared that he had killed Angus and it was at that point that all rational thoughts left his head. He didn't think to call an ambulance or seek any other form of help, he just knew that, given he had intent and the motive, there was no court in the land that wouldn't find him guilty of murder. He needed to leave. Not just this house, but the town, the city ... possibly even the country. There was nothing left for him to do.

As George ran out of the house and closed the door forcefully behind him, a sudden draught of air rushed through the lounge catching and displacing loose pieces of paper that were sitting around the room. Hence, when Angus was later discovered, sprawled out under the mantle piece, it seemed a little odd that a note from his wife lay unopened on his chest.

"Ah left that very day!" George said quietly.

"Jesus!" I gasped. "But where did you go? What about Lilly and ... ?"

"Ah didnae think of anything nor anybody but ma self!" he cut in sharply yet remorsefully. "Ah was a stupid, selfish man who couldnae even stick around to bury his own wife. Ah thought Ah hud jus' killed a man, ma wife was dead and all Ah could think aboot was the quickest way tae get tae London!"

He banged the table with his hand in a show of frustrated annoyance. It wasn't a particularly loud bang but it was enough to make the other customers in the cafe turn around. "What?" George spat, looking from person to person. Non seemed brave or bothered enough to voice an opinion and quickly went back to eating or drinking whatever it was they were eating or drinking.

I let George simmer down for a moment whilst I thought about what he had just said. I could only imagine what terrible grief and turmoil this man must have felt all those years ago (and probably still did) especially if it had affected him badly enough to leave immediately, without trace. Yes, he had taken another man's life but surely the mitigating circumstances would have shown that he wasn't of sound mind at the time of the assault? And if not? If a jury of his peers had found him guilty? Would any prison term imposed then have amounted to the metaphorical life sentence that he was serving right now? ... I think not!

I looked at George, his head bowed low as he gazed into his mug of tea and for a moment, I felt that it would best if I brought this particular rendezvous to an end. After all, the man was clearly upset and I didn't think that he needed anymore prying questions from me. But that was before my mind suddenly registered something he'd said, causing me to frown and jump right back on that train to *Question-Ville.*

"Hang on a minute," I said, causing George to look up at me with a *what now?* expression. "You just said that you *thought* you'd killed Angus?" He nodded. "But you saw him lying there, not breathing, with blood spurting out his head!" He nodded again. "So?" I encouraged.

"So what?" he replied. Infuriating man!

"So ... was he dead or not?"

"Apparently not," he answered very matter-of-factly and began to drink his tea. I waited for the unattractive slurping to subside, hoping that he would elaborate. And I waited ... and I waited some more ... and then he smiled at me and began to look out of the window. Jesus!

"George?" I urged, like a child wanting to know a secret.

"What?" he replied, turning back to me. This was starting to wind me right up!

"Angus? Not being dead?"

"Apparently not," he repeated.

'No, but you might just be if you stop there!' I thought! Talk about difficult ... sheesh! Mercifully, he didn't stop there.

28

Margaret rushed in through the front door of her home and stopped dead in her tracks, holding her hands up to her mouth in shock. "Oh ma God George," she gasped quietly. "What huv ye done?" The man responsible wouldn't answer that particular question, as the only two people present in the room now were Margaret herself and the motionless body of her husband Angus.

Margaret stood totally still staring at the figure that lay awkwardly on the lounge floor. She knew that she should be rushing over to her husband's side, taking hold of him and weeping over her second loss of the day. She knew that, at the very least, she should be phoning an ambulance or the police or somebody who would come and help. These things she knew to be the accepted norm, actions that are required and expected in such a situation. Yet, despite all that, Margaret simply couldn't move. But the fact that her legs wouldn't respond or react, wouldn't actually move wasn't her greatest concern at that moment. What was, is the fact that she really didn't want to! For somewhere deep in her sub conscious, way down in that place reserved only for suppressed anger and unspoken words, a loud and clear voice was crying out, "Serves you bloody right!"

Margaret remained perfectly still when the doctor suddenly brushed past her and went to Angus's side. She had no idea that he had followed her home and no idea that he had entered the house just a few minutes after she had.

"What's gone on here Margaret?" he asked whilst kneeling down beside Angus. When he got no reply, he looked at her and shouted her name.

Margaret was jolted harshly back into the present, blinked her eyes and then shook her head. "Ah don't know!" she half lied. She had a pretty good idea of what had gone on but rather than complicate matters, she decided to be selective with her opinion. "Ah know he hud been drinking and ... !" She paused to quickly scan the room, noticing a near empty bottle of scotch sitting on the small table by the armchair, then some disarrayed furniture, then a small patch of congealed blood on the floor by his head and then ... perfect.

The doctor noticed it as well. He frowned and picked up the small envelope that was lying on Angus's chest. Margaret braced herself. He turned it over in his hand and then held it up towards Margaret. "Is this from you?" he asked. Margaret walked over and took the envelope from the doctor's hand.

"Aye," she answered. "It's a note Ah left him tae say where Ah would be when he woke up ... but Ah left it up there!" she gestured towards the mantel piece and then looked towards his armchair. She suddenly became very nervous, hoping that what she was about to say, could be said convincingly enough for the doctor to agree with her quickly planned theory. Either that or he would know for certain that she was trying to distract his attention from what she really believed had happened here. "Maybe he got up tae read it and fell over, banging his head ... judging by that empty bottle of whisky, he was probably too drunk tae even stand up properly let alone walk!" She left it at that and waited for the doctor's response, her heart beating loudly. She hoped she had delivered the theory so that it sounded just like that, a theory not a script. She could see the doctor thinking about the possibility as he set about examining Angus but then she saw him frown when he noticed a large bruise developing on the left side of her husband's jaw.

"This looks like a ... " he began to say but was quickly interrupted by a panicking Margaret.

"He was always falling over drunk, the stupid man!" she said, dropping to her knees and placing a hand on her husband's leg. "Oh Angus!" she added sadly, for dramatic effect. What she couldn't do, was shed any tears. The doctor sighed and placed his hand on top of Margaret's but said nothing. What could he say? The woman had lost her complete family in one day and in both cases, he had been there but unable to save either of them from death. How would that look to the Coroner?

And then something extraordinary happened that completely baffled the doctor and made Margaret jump out of her skin ... Angus groaned, clearly still alive!

"Apparently, the doctor couldnae find a pulse on the bastard at first and just assumed the worst," George continued. "Bloody qwacks!" he whispered bitterly. He shook off whatever distant bad memory was about to take hold, sat up straight and smiled slightly. "Ah didnae find out till a few years later mind," he added.

"How did you find out?" I asked, thoroughly engrossed in the incredibility of it all.

"Well, there's another story," he began, showing me his empty cup and raising his eyebrows expectantly.

"Jesus," I said, smiling. "Where do you put it all? You'll be wetting your pants soon!"

"Then maybe one of those wee scones might help tae soak it up?" he suggested with a child like logic. I laughed, shook my head and went to place the order.

"So," I started, placing the tea and the scone in front of him before resuming my seat. "You were telling me how you found out about Angus?"

"Well," he said before taking a sip of his tea and flinching as the hot liquid hit his lips. "Ah hud ended up in Grimsby by then, lookin' for work on the docks or the trawlers y'know?" I nodded. "Ah've never known such an aptly named town as Grimsby!" he digressed, accentuating the word *Grim*. I smiled but quietly hoped that he would get right back on track. He did. "Anyway, Ah bumped intae this fella that used tae work on Isaac's trawler ... now, what was his name? ... Bryan or Bill or something?" He thought for a moment but then waved his hand dismissively. "Och it doesnae matter!" he continued. "So, Ah bump intae this fella, who was there lookin' fae work on the docks too ... small world eh? ... an' we get talking aboot a few things but all the time Ah'm thinkin', he looks like his seen a bloody ghost! ... really pale y'know?" He frowned, pausing to take another slurp of his tea. "So Ah said, are ye alright man 'cause ye look as white as a sheet? ... and d'ye know what he said?" I shook my head. "He looked at me straight in the eye and said, 'Ah heard ye were dead George!'"

"Why would he say that?" I asked.

"That's what Ah wanted tae know!" he replied. "So Ah asked him!"

"And what did he say?" I pushed again, trying to keep his flow going. He snorted a peculiar laugh and shook his head as if he still couldn't believe what he had been told. And after taking another mouthful of tea, he told me what Bryan or Bill or whatever his name was, had said to him.

###

Luckily for George, Angus not only made a full recovery but also claimed that he couldn't remember a thing, agreeing that he must have fallen over. He knew differently of course but would never have admitted to anybody what had actually happened that day, or why.

This was because Angus never liked being seen as a *victim* as that was akin to being weak or an *also ran* as he so eloquently put it. The rumour going round (which happened to be the truth) was that George had straightened him out after Lilly had died but the reason for the beating hadn't been clear. But, with no firm confirmation of the truth, the rumours naturally took a path of their own, developing into some of the most unlikely scenarios around. One of the more bizarre ones was that Angus was blackmailing George because he had discovered that George was homosexual; a story made more credible (in the minds of drunken men) by the fact that George and Lilly never had children. But which ever rumour was being banded about, Angus always came out looking like he was a victim and that part, in Angus's mind, needed to change. And quickly.

"So Angus?" a patron of The Jolly Piper had begun whilst sitting at the bar. "Ah heard that George knocked seven shades o' shite oot o' ye!"

"Is that so?" Angus replied, grimacing slightly.

"Aye," the man replied as the landlord place a pint in front of him. "Ah heard he beat ye so bad that ye almost died!" He lifted up his glass and held it in front of his mouth before adding. "Well, that's what Ah hear anyway!" He then took a gulp of his ale.

"Maybe ye shouldnae listen tae rumours," Angus said. "They huv a habit o' tainting the truth!"

The man thought about this for a moment. "Aye, maybe," he eventually replied, looking directly at Angus. "Cannae say Ah believed it though!"

"And why's that?" Angus asked, curiously.

The man smiled a little before replying. "Well, he's a lot smaller than ye isn't he? And Ah doubt ye would let your guard down and take that kind of beating ... no' from a boy!"

Angus knew that George wasn't a boy and certainly wasn't a lightweight by any stretch of the imagination, so he really should have ignored the comment. But there was something in this man's tone that incensed him, grated on his Karma so to speak. It sounded like this irritating man was deliberately trying to provoke him, taunt him even and to be honest, it had worked. Angus saw red. As the man began to lift his drink again, Angus took hold of his arm and slammed it back down on to the bar top, causing some of the beer to fly out of the glass. The man looked shocked. First result. Angus leant in towards the man and saw him physically flinch. Second result. "Now ye listen tae me!" the landlord growled. "Ah donae care what ye've heard from the mouths of gossip mongers but unless ye know the truth, ye keep your mouth shut in ma presence. Do Ah make ma self clear?"

"Alright, alright," The man said shakily. "Take it easy!" Angus pushed his arm away and stepped back. "Ah didnae mean anything by it Angus, jus' tellin' ye what Ah heard!"

"If ye really must know what happened," Angus said with the same bitter tone. "That little shite got what he deserved. He couldnae even look after ma daughter and now she's dead!" The man lowered his head feeling a little ashamed. He decided that he didn't want to hear Angus's story anymore but his host had other plans. Angus moved closer to the man for a second time, quickly looked around to make sure that nobody else was in earshot and lowered his voice to a near whisper. "Huv ye ever heard the expression, *he sleeps with the fishes?*"

The man frowned. "What? Like in those Mafia, Godfather films ye mean?" Angus raised his eyebrows in a *that's exactly what I mean*, way. The man stared at the landlord for a few moments longer, trying to register what it was he was saying. And then the realisation hit him causing him to gasp. "Ye mean ye've killed him!" he said a little too loudly.

"Sush man!" Angus chastised and then quickly looked around the pub again before turning back to the man. "D'ye think Ah want every man and his dog tae know?"

"But how did ye ... Ah mean when did ...?"

"That day, the day ma Lilly died," Angus continued. "The bastard broke in tae ma house an' tried tae blame me fae his neglect ... Broke in tae ma fuckin' house, can ye believe it? Anyway, he was shootin' his mouth off and ...!" He suddenly broke off, shook his head and stood back up. "Ah shouldnae be tellin' ye this!"

The man sat up straight with a look of disappointment on his face. "Eh? Listen Angus, whatever ye want tae say, ye know it'll go nae further. Ye can trust me man!"

Angus sighed and looked at him as if considering whether or not to impart this revelation. It was a ploy of course. Firstly he had wanted to make sure that his audience of one was hooked. He was. Secondly, he wanted to be sure that the man's promise of silence be as wholly beguiling as the tale itself. Oh, it would be. Now Angus could now continue revealing his *secret*, safe in the knowledge that this trustworthy citizen, this single soul of discretion, would no doubt disseminate the story to others faster than a bad pint of ale would empty your guts. He leaned towards the man for a third time. "Ah knew that George hud come tae ma house lookin' fae a fight," Angus carried on. "Drunk as ye like an' no' making any sense. But Ah jus' knew he was anglin' tae huv a go!" He paused for effect.

"So what did ye do?" the man asked eagerly.

"Well, Ah told him a few home truths fae starters but he didnae like that very much. An' then Ah told him to get oot o' ma house or Ah would throw him oot!"

"Ah bet he didnae like that either!" the man cut in and immediately received a cold stare from Angus that said, *why the fuck are you interrupting?* "Sorry Angus," he quickly added. "Carry on!"

"Well, things got very ugly Ah can tell ye!" Angus continued. "Ah went tae grab him, jus' tae escort him oot but the bastard took a swing at me! Ah managed tae avoid that one but he suddenly charged at me an' knocked me tae the ground. That's how Ah cracked ma head!" The man flinched. "Ah was dazed for a wee moment Ah can tell ye that. But Ah was up on ma feet again faster than a Jack Rabbit when he brought oot a knife ...!" Angus paused and watched as the man's eyes widened, obviously drinking it in. Another result.

The man continued to listen as Angus spun a yarn of self-defence mixed with how he was going to teach George a valuable lesson. But that wasn't enough, it seemed, as George was like a crazy rabid dog and the situation very quickly became a matter of life or death ... *kill or be killed*, as Angus reported it. "Ah knew Ah would have tae finish him ... if Ah wanted tae live that was. Ah hud nae choice!"

"How did ye do it?" The man asked. He had become very excitable, yearning for the gory details and Angus knew that his work had been done.

"That's no' important," he replied, much to the man's disappointment. "But Ah'll tell ye this," he lowered his voice even further. " Ye'll no' be seeing that fucker again!" Angus stood back again, drew a fresh pint of beer and placed it in front of his awe struck listener. "It's on the house," he said, with a slight smile. The man accepted the gift without question.

"Very kind of ye Angus," he said. "But ye donae huv tae bribe me!" he added, smiling. "You're secret's safe with me!" He tapped his nose with his finger and then raised his glass in a gratuitous yet *my lips are sealed*, kind of way. He then took a mouthful of his freebie and wondered just how long he should wait before sharing this incredible discovery with somebody else. Angus watched the man closely as he drank and wondered just how long it would take before this idiot talked.

"It wisnae too long before word got around," George said. "Which is exactly what Angus would huv wanted!"

"But why take it to that extreme?" I asked. "He could have just told the truth and have you arrested or at least have you put on the Police's wanted list for assaulting him?"

"Because that would huv made him look like a victim," George answered. "Which is what he hated. Doing it his way made him look like a man no' tae be messed with, which believe it or no', would huv given him more bargaining power with his debtors!"

I frowned, not quite understanding the rationale. "How would that work?"

"Because," George continued. "Those sort o' people rely on the element o' fear an' violence to get their money back. They're basically bullies in suits. Angus was a big man aye, but no' intimidating, if ye get what Ah mean? Nae soft, just no' intimidating. An' because he was a drunk, he always appeared tae be easy prey ... bullies love that!" He took a slurp of his tea before continuing. "But when the rumour he hud started hit the old grapevine, he was suddenly a big man with an even bigger reputation. A man with the potential tae murder anybody that pissed him off ... He'd actually become a no' right!" George twirled his finger next to his temple, indicating what a *not right* was ... I'd gotten the gist. "An' ye nae mess aboot with Glaswegian no' rights!" he added, smiling.

"But why didn't you go back and put the record straight?" I asked. "I would've done!"

George frowned. "Would ye?" he asked. It was not a question that was looking for an answer but one for me to ponder on and question my own morals. "Sometimes it's just best tae let sleeping dogs lie!"

The last adage was said quietly and more to himself than it was to me and in the silent pause for thought that followed, I suddenly got the feeling that George hadn't returned home because of some other factor in his life. Maybe he felt that, with Lilly gone, there was nothing to return home for or maybe he just thought that there was little to gain from his return other than awkward confrontation. Plausible reasons indeed but I would have placed money on them not being on his list. In fact, it actually sounded as though being *dead* in the minds of his old community suited George down to the ground and fitted in very nicely with his plans. But why? There was definitely something more to it.

"Brendan!" He suddenly and loudly announced, slapping his hand on the table and making me jump.

"Bloody hell George!" I said. "Try giving me a little notice before you shout out. You scared the crap out of me!" He chortled a small apology but as he took a further mouthful of his beverage, I could have sworn I heard him mutter something that sounded very much like *ponce.* "Who's Brendan anyway?" I asked.

"He's the fella Ah met in Grimsby," he replied.

"Oh right," I remarked. "So glad I nearly had a heart attack hearing that revelation!"

"Ah donae know why Ah couldnae remember his name," he continued, oblivious to my sarcasm. "Christ, why did Ah no' remember that? ... stupid!"

To me, it sounded like he was being a little harsh on himself and I told him as much. And then he revealed that Brendan was actually Margaret's younger brother aka Lilly's uncle. Okay, maybe he should have remembered that? But again, I assured him that everybody forgets people's names from time to time (even relatives) and at least he got there in the end. But George just wouldn't let it go as if forgetting his name was like forgetting an important moment in history or a personal anniversary or something. It wasn't until George told me about the other news that Brendan had imparted on the day that they met, that I could fully understand why it was so important to him. *Something else on his mind?* I had thought minutes earlier. My God there was! And though I had suspected it, I would never have come close to guessing exactly what it was.

You see, not only was Brendan Lilly's Uncle ... and therefore a kind of direct physical link to her memory ... but somebody much more important than that. Brendan, it turned out, was also the Great Uncle and Godfather of a little girl named Sarah ... aka, the only child of George and Lilly Bell.

29

On the 4th August 1970, Lillian Bell used every last ounce of breath and energy in her fragile body to give birth to a baby girl. But that wasn't enough.

"Is the baby okay?" she asked through tears and shortness of breath. "Please, tell me the baby is okay!" She needed to know. In spite of what she knew was now inevitable, she had to be sure that her gift to George was perfect, before that inevitability arrived.

"It's a girl!" the doctor announced solemnly, unable to disguise the concern in his voice. Cutting the umbilical cord with some urgency, he picked the baby up and turned towards the midwife standing behind him, a smile on her face and a soft, warm towel in her hands in which to wrap the new born child. Her smile quickly dissipated when she saw the doctor's pained expression.

"Is ... she ... alright ... doctor?" Lilly panted. The pain she was feeling at that moment was excruciating and relentless, surging through her body with neither remorse nor compassion. She had to fight it. She clenched her fists so tightly that her nails dug deep into the palms of her hands causing small trickles of blood to appear. "Doctor?" she asked again in a near whisper. Margaret gently dabbed her daughter's brow desperately wanting to offer some words of comfort. But when she opened her mouth to speak, nothing would come out. And why would it? What possible reassurances could she give Lilly at this moment that could be said with total conviction? She closed her mouth and bowed her head.

Behind them, both the doctor and the midwife huddled around the newly delivered child, clearing her mouth and nose of fluids brought from within the womb and gently smacked her bottom. The method used to make baby's cry and allow their small lungs to taste their first breath of life, had no effect. The midwife tried again but this time held the child upside down and smacked a little harder. Nothing. The doctor tried vigorously rubbing and massaging the child's chest, he tried compressions and mouth to mouth, he tried whatever armoury he had within his medical knowledge to evoke a heart beat. Still nothing. He opened the child's eyelids to check the tiny pupils beneath before finally looking up at his colleague, shaking his head. The midwife saw the pools within his eyes, causing tears of her own to form and then track slowly down her cheeks. Doctor McKay felt helpless ... no ... useless! And now he had to tell a mother how useless he was that he couldn't even save her daughter. What made the whole situation worse was the fact that Lilly had very little time of her own left. She had taken everything that her petite body could endure and then some. But the massive blood loss coupled with an extremely difficult birth had taken its toll and simply put her beyond the point of no return.

He had told Lilly earlier that he doubted he would be able to save both her and the child and strongly advised against continuing the birth.

"Lilly," He had started softly whilst holding her hand. "Ye huv lost a lot of blood and Ah don't know how much more your body can take!" He glanced across at the midwife and then back to Lilly. "Look. An ambulance is on its way but ye are too weak tae be moved tae a hospital. And even if ye could be, there's no' enough time!" He sighed and squeezed her hand a little more tightly. "If ye huv this bairn, Ah'm no' sure that *ye* will survive the trauma of it all, let alone the child. Let me just concentrate on fixing you?" He thought that she would accept his advice, allowing him to save one life at least ... he was wrong.

She stared at him through tired, dull eyes and attempted to smile. The beads of sweat that peppered the grey pallor of her face, seem to twinkle like precious gems whenever the light caught them but it did little to disguise the fact that she now bore the look of a woman twice her age. Any outsider suddenly entering the room would have put money on the lady in the bed being in her eighties and expecting the imminent arrival of death. Lilly grimaced as she attempted to shift her weight slightly but her exhausted body wouldn't even allow her to do that and she flopped back into the same position with a pained wheeze. Taking a few moments to compose herself again, her dry and cracked lips curled back into a thin but kind smile just before she spoke.

"Ah know you're doing your best doctor," she whispered. "But Ah also know what's next for me and nothing in that wee black bag of yours is going tae stop it!" The doctor glanced at his medical bag on the chest of drawers next to the bed. Deep down, he knew that Lilly was probably right but he refused to let that sentiment rise to the surface.

"Don't say that Lilly! " Margaret pleaded. "Ye cannae ..."

"Please mum," Lilly cut in. "Let the doctor save our baby!" The doctor stared at her, quickly trying to think of an appropriate response; a solution or an alternative perhaps ... he couldn't. "It's okay. Really!" Lilly added softly, as though sensing his dilemma. "Just let George be the daddy he has always wanted tae be ... please!"

###

'Is she alright doctor?' Those words of fearful anticipation echoed around the doctor's head time and time again as if branded into his conscience ... He couldn't move as anguish gripped his body, seemingly locking his joints. How could he turn around and tell this woman of her loss? How could he look her in the eye and tell her that the baby she had probably traded her own life for, was dead? He felt sick to his stomach. Lilly had fought hard to hold on to the last moments of her own life yet those last moments would now be spent grieving over the death of a child she had waited so long to bear. He had spent all of his years on this earth believing and hoping that there was a God but now, he wasn't so sure.

And then, in between that split moment of finding the courage to face Lilly and actually turning around to do it, something happened that was nothing short of miraculous ... the small, lifeless form that was lay in front of him suddenly gasped, juddered and then exhaled. The doctor and midwife stood open-mouthed staring down at the little girl who had now, in her own time, decided to start living. No tears, no fuss, just the methodical, gentle sound of breathing coupled with a steady return of colour. The doctor quickly listened to

185

her chest, checked her other vital signs and then, after a dumbfounded sigh, allowed himself a very large smile. The midwife was still weeping, only now it was with joy and relief. The doctor almost followed suit. Instead, he turned around to Lilly and was pleased to announce. "She's perfect Lilly. Just perfect!"

Lilly smiled as her baby was placed into her arms and for the first time in many hours, all the pain, all the anguish she had felt, was gone. Her face had the expression of someone who had just become content with life after accomplishing a very difficult task, making even the doctor think that she looked surprisingly *well*.

Margaret held on to her daughter's hand, pulling it up to her own mouth to kiss it. She smiled through her tears but couldn't hide the sadness that was tearing her apart. Despite the miracle that was her granddaughter and despite the sudden illusion of health on Lilly's face, Margaret knew that her daughter was about to leave her.

"It's alright now mum," Lilly whispered. "Please don't cry!"

It was a request that Margaret couldn't fulfil. "Ah love you so much Lilly!" she trembled.

"Ah know," Lilly replied softly. "An Ah love you too!" She squeezed her mother's hand tenderly. "Look after George for me ... and Sarah!" Margaret frowned slightly. "After Grandma!" Lilly added seeing her mother's confusion.

Margaret began to cry again and quickly took hold of her daughter in a warm embrace, kissing her on the cheek. Before she pulled away, she whispered into her ear. "Ah promise sweetheart!"

And then, Lilly looked down at her own daughter and kissed her on the forehead. "You're ma special girl," she whispered. "And you always will be ... Ah love you so much!" As hard as she found it, Lilly beckoned the midwife over to take her daughter from her before turning once more to her own mother. "Ah'm ready now mum," she said softly.

Margaret nodded slightly and stroked her daughter's face. "Sleep well darling," she trembled and kissed her daughter once more. Lilly smiled at her mother and mouthed the words *I love you.*

On 4th August 1970, Lillian Bell closed her eyes for the final time.

George dabbed his eyes with a tissue ... as did I.

"Ah know it's difficult tae understand," he said after a short pause. "But Ah was so full of grief, so full of anger, that Ah saw nothing but ma wife in that room!" I tried to offer him a reassuring yet understanding smile but it served no purpose. "And Ah was so bloody consumed with vengeance," he continued. "Ah didnae even stop tae find out what she hud given me ... what she hud given her life for!"

I gave George a couple minutes before I finally asked. "Why didn't you go back when you found out about Sarah?"

He shrugged his shoulders. "Ah thought she would be better off without me," he replied genuinely. "And donae forget," he added. "Ah was suppose tae be dead!"

There was a long silence between George and I whilst we dwelled on the story that he had just shared. I wondered how he really felt, knowing that he had a daughter but had never even seen her. Wasn't he curious? Didn't he want to know what she looked like or how she had turned out? I know that if it were my daughter, I'd have wanted to know! Did he even know where she was?

And then, like a voice of reason, somebody sitting behind George unexpectedly spoke, directing their comment towards him. "You need to find her!"

We both looked towards the source of the voice and stared in utter disbelief when we discovered who had spoken with such authority on the matter. The teenage waitress, who was more adept at giving attitude rather than advice, sat there holding a tissue in one hand and a mug of what appeared to be hot chocolate in the other. She stared at us through reddened eyes and shrugged. "Just saying," she added, softly. "Otherwise, you'll regret it big time!"

She then got up and sloped off into the kitchen without another word, leaving two extremely stunned men in her wake. George turned back to me and shook his head. "Can ye believe it?" he said, half amused, half annoyed. "She was bloody ear wiggin'!"

I also shook my head in disbelief though as much as it grieved me, I had to admit that she had a valid point. "Maybe she's right," I offered. "Maybe you should try and find her!"

George looked at me with that now familiar *I've got something to tell you* look. And for the second time in as many minutes, my mouth dropped open with utter surprise as the aged Scot quietly declared: "No need son ... she's here in Manchester!"

###

30

Just when I thought that I had got the measure of George, he'd come up with yet another surprise. Discovering that his daughter now resided and worked in Manchester would explain a lot though. It was the reason that he had come to this fair city in the first place apparently, finding out some years ago that Sarah had cut loose from Glasgow and now worked for a firm of solicitor's based here. Was this the reason he sometimes sloped off to one of his many *appointments* during our chats? I didn't know for sure but I was about to find out.

"It was nineteen ninety-eight when Ah found out that she was here," he began to explain. "Ah was in Liverpool, drifting between low paid, part time work and the streets but when Ah heard she was so close, Ah jumped the first train here and huv been here ever since!"

I nodded and then smiled as I remembered the day I first met George and how he had produced a 1998 diary ... I guess I now knew the significance.

"Finding out where she worked was a bloody nightmare though!" he chuckled. "Do ye know how many firms of solicitor's there are in the centre of Manchester?"

"Quite a few I would imagine!" I replied.

"Two hundred and thirty five!" he exclaimed in a high-pitched tone.

"Wow!" I gasped. "How the hell did you find out where she worked amongst all those?"

George tapped his temple and smiled. "No' just a pretty face me son!" he said proudly, although I secretly disputed that particular accolade. "Y'see," he continued. "Ah knew that she was a corporate solicitor, no' criminal, right!"

"Pity," I interrupted, smiling. "It would have been ideal for your recent episode with the cops!"

George just stared at me with that *what a pillock* look on his face. "D'ye want tae hear this or no'?" he said with a slight scolding tone in his voice.

My face reddened and yet again, I felt like my dad was chastising me. "Yes ... sorry George ... carry on!"

"Right. So Ah concentrated on the one's that just did corporate law and that narrowed it down tae seventy five within the city centre!"

"How did you manage to sort them all out?" I asked, genuinely intrigued as to how he had become a seemingly adept detective. It's not like he would have had easy access to the internet or anything, not in 1998 anyway.

"Ah used the phone book mainly," he replied. "Ninety nine per cent of them have free phone numbers, so it cost me nothing tae ring them. The one's that were no' free, Ah visited in person!"

"God. That must have taken you ages!" I gasped.

"Near on a month!" he said, again with a proud tone. "But Ah got there in the end!" He sat back in his chair and took on a thoughtful moment. He then smiled to himself and gave a peculiar nod as though he was approving of something ... or someone.

"What?" I asked, with an inquisitive frown.

He looked up at me with the same smile on his face. "She's a senior partner ye know?"

I didn't, but I smiled back and found myself giving the same peculiar nod of approval. "You must be very proud?" I offered.

"Aye," he replied. "That Ah am!"

And then something occurred to me. How did he know that his daughter had come down to Manchester? And why had he gone to all that trouble to find out where she worked when he didn't even return to Scotland once he'd heard about her actual existence? Was he planning on turning up at her office or had he already done that? I assumed that there was more mystery to uncover here, some further revelations that George had not yet imparted but would suddenly reveal and embroil me, once more, in his world of adventure.

As it happened, the answer was quite simple and not very adventurous at all but it did fill me with a touch of sorrow when he explained the *whys* and *where for's* of how he managed to keep a track of Sarah.

"Ye already know that two people knew Ah wisnae dead, right?" George asked.

"Yes," I replied. "Angus, obviously and then Brendan!"

George nodded. "Well, when Ah saw Brendan that day, he wisnae just surprised by the fact that Ah was alive, he was surprised by the fact that Margaret hud been right aboot me all along!" I raised my eyebrows. "Aye. Margaret knew as well?" he added, seeing my look and sensing my next question. "Apparently, she kept telling him that Ah was still alive but he hudnae really paid much attention tae her, especially as he wholly believed the rumour that Angus hud spun!"

"But if Margaret knew," I began. "Why didn't she put everybody straight?"

George sighed and shook his head. "Because Angus hud developed intae a nastier bastard than he ever was and giving Margaret a crack for saying something out of turn hud turned intae the norm rather than the exception!" I saw George grimace and clench his fists. "He also told her that if anybody ever found out that Ah was alive, or if Ah ever returned, he would huv me arrested and personally make sure that Sarah was taken in tae care!"

"Jesus!" I exclaimed. "He really didn't like you did he? What a psycho!!"

George nodded again. "Anyway," he continued. "Long story short, Ah telephoned Margaret that day and we kept in touch right up until nineteen ninety eight. It's because of her that Ah got tae know how ma daughter was getting on!" George sighed and I saw his eyes glaze slightly. "The day after she told me that Sarah hud moved tae Manchester, Ah heard that she ... well, she ..." George broke off and gave a heavy sigh of sadness. He shook his head and rubbed his face with his hands, trying to regain his composure. I automatically understood what he was trying to say and knew that I needed to keep my counsel. This wasn't the time for pushing or prying, it was the time to let George have his minute of silence. "Ah knew she'd been unwell fae some time," he continued quietly. "But it was jus' so sudden, like she ... och Ah don't no!"

"Like she what?" I asked.

George looked directly at me with slatted eyes as though considering how to present his thoughts. "It was like she hud done what she needed tae do y'know? She hud brought ma daughter up almost single handed ... protected her, cared for her and loved her like a mother would ... but when Sarah finally *fled the nest* so tae speak, Margaret must huv felt that her work was done. When Sarah was with her, she hud a purpose in life, a purpose that outweighed her sham of a marriage. When Sarah left, Margaret had nothing more tae look forward tae, save a few beatings from a drunken bully! ... Ah think she jus' decided tae give up living!"

If George was right, it made for a horrible ending to the existence of such a nice person and although it was only a theory, it was obvious that George had convinced himself that this was the only explanation for the passing of Margaret. My own thoughts were that George had developed this theory as a result of the guilt he felt for not being in Sarah's life. Margaret had probably passed away due to her age and her ailments but George would never have accepted that. He would sooner carry the burden of a self-proclaimed responsibility for her death ... like a punishment he felt he deserved ... rather than except what was more likely to be the truth. He needed to rid himself of his angst and, as the seed of an idea entered my head, I believed that I might just be the man for the job.

"I'm guessing that you have seen Sarah whilst she's been in Manchester?" I asked. George looked at me with a frown as though I had stumbled on something top secret. I smiled back at him. "Given what you have just told me George, I surmised that the frequent *appointments* you are always scuttling off to aren't with your financial advisor?" George shrugged. "And I further surmise that even though you know where she works and have no doubt watched her leave her office to go to lunch or home or whatever, you haven't actually spoken to her yet, have you?"

"Ye sound like one of those poncey court barristers with all your surmising!" he answered grumpily. "And no Perry bloody Mason, Ah huvnae spoken to her. If ye were a respectable business woman, would ye want some scruffy street bum like me coming up tae ye saying, *hello there love, Ah'm yer dad*?" My face must have said it all. "No. Ah didnae think so. And who would? Look at the state o' me!" he said, sounding both embarrassed and annoyed. " Plus," he continued. "Ye seem tae forget that she thinks Ah am dead!"

"But you're not are you George?" I said with a small, frustrated snap. "And I think she might like to know that, don't you? I know I would!"

"Ye huvnae a bloody clue man!" George spat back defensively and quickly stood up. "Ye'll be tellin' me she has rights next!"

"Well I think she has a right to know, yes!" I said. George scowled at me then stomped off towards the cafe door. "But if I'm being honest," I shouted after him, quickly. "I think she might have an idea that you're still alive anyway!"

George stopped mid exit, turned around and let out a snort that sounded a little like a bull about to attack a red rag. "And how the hell did ye come tae that conclusion?"

I looked around the cafe and noticed that the other patrons, of which there were half a dozen or so, had suddenly put their own business on hold and were now taking an avid interest in ours. You know when you see a married couple that are about to have a row and wifey looks a little embarrassed by it all? Well that's how I suddenly felt. I glanced at the waitress, who was also more interested in our affairs than what she was paid to do and produced an unusual nervy grin that I could only liken to a plasticine bloke called Wallace. She raised her eyebrows and shook her head slowly in that all too familiar *you've upset him again* way, before turning her back

---

193

on me. I stood up in a huff, grabbed my coat off the back of the chair and headed for the door ... the door that George was still blocking incidentally. "Let's take this outside George!" I said, though the tone in which I said it came out slightly wrong.

George's eyes widened "Oh aye?" he rasped, pushing his chest out.

"Not for a fight you great lump," I quickly added with a nervous chortle whilst clapping him on his arm. "So we can talk without an audience!" I gestured towards the people sat around the greasy tables still watching on and noticed that some bloke had stood up and was mid-way through putting his raincoat on. He looked at me with a frown, tutted, removed his coat and resumed his seat. If I didn't know any better, I'd have said that he was planning to follow us out in the hope of watching a scrap ... unbelievable! I sighed and looked back at George. "That ok with you?" I asked.

"Ah suppose!" George replied curtly, before walking outside. Now, maybe it was just me, but I could have sworn that I saw the same look of disappointment on George's face that I saw on raincoat man's ... again, unbelievable!

We managed to find an unoccupied bench in Piccadilly Gardens that wasn't decorated with half empty chips 'n' gravy trays or freshly laid pigeon crap and sat down. Despite the absence of discarded rubbish on our particular seat, it was impossible not to notice the odour of stale urine mixed with old, alcohol-infused vomit and it made me grimace.

"What's wrong with ye now!" George asked, obviously noticing my look.

I looked around the *gardens* shaking my head at the irony of it all. To any outsider, the very name, *Piccadilly Gardens,* must have conjured up a vision of beautiful flowers and trees blended with a summer fresh aroma that wafts gently across beautifully manicured lawns. The reality? ... "It looks like a shit hole and it smells like a shit hole!" I eventually answered. "They should have named it Piccadilly Garbage!"

"Ha ha ... welcome tae ma world!" George tittered softly. After a moments silence, he turned to me with an unusual expression on his face. It was a look of mild excitement mixed with a little curiosity, dusted with a sprinkling of frustration. It's how I would imagine a young boy might look on his birthday, when he desperately wants to open his presents but at the same time, he desperately needs to go to the toilet. For a grown man, it was a strange look. But I also saw something else residing in his eyes that was totally unmistakeable ... a glimmer of hope. But what was he hoping for? I had absolutely no idea ... not at that point anyway.

"So Perry," he began. "What makes ye think that Sarah suspects Ah'm no' dead? ... it's no' like ye have spoken tae her or even seen her fae that matter!"

"Well firstly," I began. "You can cut out the *Perry* crap!" He smiled. "And secondly," I continued. "If everything you have told me about Margaret is true and ..."

"Why wouldn't it be?" George interrupted, frowning.

"And ... " I repeated, accentuating the word. " ... I've no reason to think otherwise, then I would put money on her having at least hinted to Sarah that you weren't dead!" George frowned again and pulled his chin in towards his chest in a *what you talking about?* way. "Look George," I said. "Margaret thought the world of you yes?" He shrugged. "And given what she went through ... losing Lilly and being married to the wrong man and everything ... I reckon she would have wanted to share more than just memories of you with her granddaughter. What I'm trying to say, is that Sarah was last in a line of everything that was good in Margaret's life ... Isaac, Lilly, you. Without her, she'd have nobody. I reckon she wouldn't have relished the prospect of Sarah ending up with no family like she had and that's why I think she may just have told her that you are in fact still alive. Think about it. Why would Margaret let somebody she loved so much grow up believing that they were an orphan when they weren't? Not her style I would say!"

George pondered on this for a while, running his hand through the thick white whiskers on his chin. And then he came up with one of the most ridiculous questions I have ever heard him ask. "But, if she knows that Ah'm alive, then why has she no' tried tae find me?"

I sighed. "George, George! ... One, as you have already pointed out, I have never spoken to her, so I wouldn't know if she has or she hasn't. Two, you've never spoken to her so you don't know either and three, you live on the bloody streets of Manchester so I'm guessing you ain't in the phone book!"

"Aye alright smart arse," George rebuked. "So what do you *surmise* that Ah should do?"

Nice sarcasm I thought ... again! Yet the moment he said it, that glimmer of hope I had seen in his eyes minutes earlier, not only returned but also intensified to a positive sparkle. I stared at him thinking about my answer when something suddenly occurred to me. I was wrong about that sparkle. It wasn't a look of hope I saw, not at all. It was the look of somebody yearning to be encouraged to do something that they are afraid to do ... George actually wanted, nay, needed my encouragement! When we were in the cafe, pre walking out, I had an idea in my head and now, sat on this crummy bench, George was actually handing me a plate of opportunity on which to put that idea. How he would feel about my idea though, was another matter entirely! I smiled at him. "George old boy," I began. "It's time to trust Perry!"

###

31

It was one of the most miserable pre-winter Thursdays that I have ever known. During the previous night's news bulletin, the weather man had assured the nation that it was going to be a crisp yet bright Autumnal day with little chance of rain ... I guess he was talking about another country 'cause on the 20th of November 2008 in Manchester, UK, it was grey, bitterly cold and poured down with a vengeance.

As I trudged my way through the city to where I'd hoped George would be, I couldn't help but feel a touch apprehensive about how the day would pan out. Just over a week earlier, I had set about putting a plan into action, though trying to convince George to get on board was another matter.

###

"Tell me ye're no' bein' serious?" George gasped.

"Never been more serious in my life," I replied. "And if you think about it, it's the only way forward ... unless you want to spend the rest of your life being miserable and living with *what if's*?" My suggestion that he should actually approach and introduce himself to Sarah rather than watch her from a safe distance, had not been received with much enthusiasm.

George thought about it for a moment and then shook his head. "Ah cannae do it man!" he said.

Now. The thing that I'd learnt about George from our many meetings is that when he said certain things, you knew exactly where he stood. He was strong willed, opinionated and for the most part, immovable from his decisions, no matter how stubborn his decisions sometimes appeared to be. The other thing I had learnt about George, is that when he said something without full conviction (like now) he was either unsure that his decision was correct or just needed a little encouragement to make the right decision.

"Why can't you do it? Are you afraid?" I asked, not quite walking the path of encouragement just yet. You'd have thought that I had actually called him a *chicken shit* such was the way he spat back his reply.

"What? ... Ah'm no' bloody afraid of anything man!" he snapped.

"Ok then ... so why won't you do it?"

"Why do ye think?" he replied with a rhetoric tone, as if the answer was glaringly obvious. "Look at the state of me!" He opened his arms, inviting me to look at his attire. "Ah'm a bloody mess!" he added, he too now looking down at his clothes. When he looked back up at me, his eyes had become sad. "Would ye want someone like me coming up tae ye and announcing that Ah was yer father?" he offered, quietly. I didn't reply immediately. "Ye'd huv nothing tae do with me would ye?" he continued. "And who could blame ye? Who'd want tae huv a bloody tramp as a father?"

"George ..." I started, but he held his hand up to stop me from saying anything further.

"If she doesnae see me, then she cannae hate me," he said. "And though it may be hard for ye tae believe son, Ah still huv some dignity left ... donae make me lose that too!"

As George looked away from me to enter the world of *feeling sorry for yourself,* I had already begun to think of the options. I wasn't going to allow the old boy to give up so easily, especially as I was in no doubt that having the opportunity to speak to Sarah was something he yearned to do. He hadn't actually said as much, no, but I knew I was right. To me, the main sticking point in this scenario wasn't that George was afraid, it was the fact that he was embarrassed about his appearance. And that readers, is something I knew could be fixed. "Right George," I began, now running up the path of encouragement and enthusiasm. "Here's what you and I are going to do!" I reached into my coat pocket just as George turned back to face me, frowning and ready to object. It was amazing how quickly he lost that frown when he saw me produce and then open my wallet.

###

So there I was, stood in the fire exit doorway of some nameless, grey building on Mosley Street trying to save myself from becoming completely drenched. Apart from smelling like an overused urinal, the alcove served the purpose well and also gave me a fairly good vantage point from which to try and spot George. The only downside was that I would have had to lean back out into the rain if I wanted to see to my immediate right or left. I'd hoped that wouldn't be necessary.

It was one o'clock in the afternoon, the start of the lunchtime hour in the city and the street was mobbed with people scurrying back and forth like frightened mice. Whether this illusion of panic was down to the citizens of Manchester merely trying to escape the relentless, icy downpour of the day or whether they were just rushing to take their place in the seemingly infinite queue that always develops in Gregg's the Bakers, I didn't know for sure. What I did know, is that their want to remain dry or their need to secure that last cheese and onion pasty did nothing to help me spot George, as it appeared that everyone was wearing the same grey coat and had the same black umbrella or sodden newspaper above their heads ... it was an ocean of faceless people.

I checked my watch and cursed the fact that ten minutes had already passed from our agreed meeting time. Flashbacks of the first meet up with George entered my head and a small seed of irritation began to germinate. After a further five minutes, this had changed into a flowering bud of doubt and I hoped for two things. The first was that he hadn't lost his

199

bottle and the second was that we hadn't missed our opportunity if it turned out that he was just late.

I was standing across from where George reliably informed me that Sarah worked and already, streams of employees had left the building in search of lunch. Having no idea what his daughter looked like (despite me constantly second guessing every eligible female that came out of the doors) I would never know if she had come out or not. "Where the bloody hell are you George?" I muttered to myself, scanning the sea of chaos before me. To get a better view, I leant out from the doorway, quickly looked to my right and then to my left and then leant back in again. I sighed and brushed the renewed coating of wet from my hair, just as my brain suddenly decoded an image that my eyes had sent it. I frowned, thought about what I might just have seen, shook my head, dismissed it and then considered it again, all within two seconds. *'Surely not?'* I thought, questioning my senses. Reservations aside, I leaned out of my haven for a second time and focused on an area not fifty feet from where I was standing. I looked, I saw and then, I smiled. For there, poking out of a doorway identical to the one that I was standing in, was the unmistakeable sight of a bright blue, polka dotted panel of a lady's umbrella ... aka George's umbrella.

I took the plunge, stepped out from my shelter and headed towards the crazy blue beacon, shoulders hunched and chin down as I attempted to prevent the rain from cutting my face in half. But as I got closer to the man holding the brolly, I suddenly stopped in my tracks, puzzled "Oh crap!" I whispered to myself whilst frowning. "It's not George!" I truly thought that I had suffered a case of mistaken identity and almost turned back around and walked away. What prevented me from doing this was the fact that the man holding the brolly, saw me and offered up a small wave. I squinted, frowned again and then became wide-eyed with surprise. It was remarkable yet indescribably weird. For, the tramp with the scruffy, dirty clothes, wild hair and crazy beard that I had come to know and love, had now been replaced with a new suited, freshly trimmed, clean looking man that wouldn't have been out of place in a Burton's shop window ... apart from the brolly that is! ... oh and the red tie!

"Wow George," I exclaimed, when I was standing next to him. "Looking fly my man!"

"Ah've no bloody idea what that means," he responded with a slight smile. "But Ah hope it means that Ah look ok?"

"You look better than ok. You look like a completely different person!" And he did. A three quarter length raincoat over a smart single-breasted suit, both grey; new shoes, black; a crisp shirt with cufflinks, white and ... well, we know about the tie don't we? Both his hair and beard had been cut into short, clean-line styles which, together with his weathered yet tanned face, gave him the look of a Sean Connery meets Giorgio Armani kind of mix. Amazing. And then something occurred to me. How did he manage to achieve this new look on the mere fifty pounds that I had given to him during our last encounter? The suit alone must have set him back near on a hundred quid, if not more!

I had advised him ten days previously (despite his grumbling resistance) to get himself a haircut and a shave and use the facilities of either the YMCA or the Samaritans' hostel to take a shower. I also suggested that he buy a new shirt, ditch the overcoat and generally make himself a bit more presentable. "At least give yourself a fighting chance George," I had said. "First impressions count and all that!" He had eventually agreed and though I had shown as much faith and enthusiasm in him as I possibly could have (and tipped him the cash) I didn't hold out much hope of a spellbinding transformation. How wrong was I?

"You need to tell me where you shop George," I said. "'Cause I could do with getting a two hundred pound set of threads for a mere fifty quid!" I smiled and looked him up and down inquisitively. He shifted uneasily on his feet and tried to change the subject, making me even more determined to find out how he had managed to acquire such a collection. "George?" I started, elongating his name in a *what you been up to* tone. "Is there something you would like to tell me?"

Eventually he did tell me and though what he had done was clearly wrong, I had to admire the barefaced cheek of the man. For an old man living on the streets, he was certainly resourceful, even if it did mean that he occasionally broke the law.

Now, I won't divulge the name of the premises but there is a particular department store in the city (George reliably informs me) where one of the cubicles in the men's changing area is situated right next to an unalarmed, emergency exit door. George also informed me that within that particular cubicle, somebody, sooner or later, would discover a discarded pile of old and dirty clothes. They might even put two and two together and realise what had actually happened, though George doubted that. "It's no' changed in the five years since Ah last did it!" He pointed out with some authority and a wry smirk. "But some never learn!" When I attempted to point out the error of his ways he merely shrugged his shoulders in a *serves them right* sort of way before nonchalantly mumbling something about them being insured. "An' they shouldn't be so stupid," he added, as an afterthought. "Ah mean, who puts a cubicle right next tae a way out anyway? A recipe fae trouble if ye ask me!"

When I launched into a little lecture on honesty and integrity, George looked out across the street and I suspected that my words were probably falling on deaf ears, especially the one that was now facing me ... ignorance is not a virtue George!

Despite his refusal to acknowledge what I had to say, I carried on regardless, not ready to step down off my soapbox just yet. However, mid way through my sermon (and without looking at me) George suddenly reached out and grabbed my arm causing me to stop way short of the finale. "What the ...?" I began, staring at his gripping hand before tracking up to his face in search of an explanation.

The explanation I sought came both immediately and proudly as George gestured with his head and duly announced the sighting of his daughter ... And then, the rain stopped.

###

32

More often than not, when I'm reading a book, I tend to visualise what the characters in that book would look like in real life. To me, it makes the story more enjoyable and adds a touch of realism for the time that I spend immersed in a novel. Sometimes (if it's a story I really like) I like to consider which actors would play which parts if the book were ever made into a film. Perhaps this is something you do? Perhaps, like me, you have read a couple of the *Harry Potter* books prior to the movie releases and imagined what *Hermione Granger* or *Ron Weasley* would look like if you met them? Perhaps you have also read a novel by Stephen King or Jeffrey Archer or whoever and thought of the characters, '*I know who would be great in that part*'? This happens because the author has done their job well, included good descriptive texts and laid the foundations on which the reader can build their imagination. Without it, the reader's mind has no point of reference from which to work and so the subconscious begins to conjure up all sorts of variables based on what you think rather than what you know. Confused? Well, here's a prime example to help you out ...

Up until the point of me actually seeing Sarah in the flesh, so to speak, I came to realise that George, since I found out that he had a daughter, had never described what she looked like. And so, as a result of that missing foundation block, my subconscious had created an image of its own and to be frank readers, it wasn't good.

Now, seeing as my point of *descriptive reference* could only be based on her father's looks, I had imagined Sarah to be a female version of George ... sternly built, not particularly attractive, little if any make-up, difficult hair and perhaps a faint yet noticeable *lady-tash* developing above her top lip. During business hours, I envisaged her wearing a frumpy, pale blue twinset with matching skirt that was both out-dated and a size too small for her frame to fit comfortably into. For leisure, she would wear a thick knitted jumper, dark green slacks and walking boots. I believed that she lived on her own with her dogs (long-haired whatever's that moulted on everything) in a small, musty smelling house full of cheap bric-a-brac that she had purchased from car boot sales and church jumbles. She ate soup, drank leafed tea (never bags), knitted stuff and listened to the news on Radio 4. By ten o'clock every night, she would be in her bed covered by thick, brown blankets (not a duvet) and would be reading some obscure novel by the light of a forty watt, pink shaded, bedside lamp, whilst her dogs lay at her feet noisily licking their privates before settling down ... All this because George had neglected to paint me a picture!

In reality though, I couldn't have been more wrong about her appearance and if I tell you that I could imagine *Joley Richardson* or *Kate Winslet* playing her part in a film, then you might just get a sense of how incredibly off the mark I had been.

She was tall and slender (though not skinny) with the well-fitted, dark trouser suit she was wearing, giving her a look of class and confidence. It also brought out the best of her figure without being overly sexual ... there was nothing frumpy about this woman. Her shoulder length hair, a lighter shade of chestnut, fell stylishly about her face, emphasising her high cheek bones and a complexion that was strikingly pale ... not in an *ill-looking* way but in a way that made you believe that Mother Nature had designed it so, to accentuate her natural beauty. Even at the distance from where we watched her, I could see that she had inherited her father's eyes, such was the intensity of the blue. As for the natural beauty part? ... I guess that had come from her mother's side. Sorry George!

And from what I could see, I was right about one thing though. She wore little or no make-up. And why would she? You wouldn't add a coating of emulsion to a Van Gogh would you? Sometimes, things are better just left untouched. That was Sarah.

###

So. Before this little rendezvous, I had formulated a bit of a plan and no matter how basic or how bare the bones of that particular plan might have been, it was still a plan. The premise was simple. Convince Georgie boy that he needed to speak to his daughter ... check ... get him to spruce up a little ... massive check ... and then arrange a day to put the rest of my plan into action ... thrice check.

Trouble was, that's as far as my master plan stretched. I hadn't really given much consideration to what we would do when we actually saw Sarah, putting my faith into the time honoured, *we'll cross that bridge when we come to it,* routine. In retrospect, it was a pretty stupid leap of faith given the fact that that was the whole point of being outside her office in the first place. And now, here we were and there she was, standing a mere seventy-five feet away from us on the opposite side of the street. If I mentioned that I was feeling a little apprehensive about how the day would pan out, well strike that, because at this juncture, I was feeling as nervous as hell ... and George wasn't any bloody help either!

We were just standing there, frozen to the spot and open mouthed with absolutely no idea of what we were going to do next. We were bordering on looking pathetic to be frank.

"What now?" George suddenly asked, though his tone was more akin to one awaiting instruction from a leader rather than a general open question.

"Huh?" I replied, turning towards him, a little taken aback. "What do you mean, '*what now*'? ... How should I know?"

George glared at me. "What do ye mean, '*how should ye know*'? This was your bloody idea!"

"Yeah, but she's your bloody daughter!"

"No shite Sherlock! But what should Ah do?"

"Well ... maybe you should go and talk to her?"

"What? Jus' like that?"

"Yes, why not?

"Jus' like that?"

"Who are you, Tommy bleeding Cooper? ... Yes. Just like that!"

"Now?"

"No George, sometime next month! Of course *now!* Not afraid are you?"

"Wouldn't ye be?"

"Who me? Ha. No way. Not afraid of anythi ... Oh shit, she's crossing over!"

"Oh Shite ... what now?"

"Stop asking me, *what now!*"

"Och no! ... she's walking away!"

"Then stop her!"

"How?"

"I don't know! ... Call her!"

"What?"

"You heard. Call her ... now!"

"But ... Ah cannae!"

"Jesus George! ... SARAH!!"

"Shush! ... What ye doing man?"

"Re-uniting the pair of you ... SARAH, SARAH BELL!"

George was about to protest for a second time but it was too late. Sarah had already turned around and was now staring at the pair of us, frowning.

And then, I did something that *was* pathetic ... I gave her the most supercilious smile that my panicking brain could muster and actually waved at her ... not a stern, open-palmed gesture of the *'hello, it was me that just called your name, please give me a minute of your time'* kind of wave, oh no! It was a limp wristed, rapid fire, *'look at me, I'm grannie from the '70s TV show, The Beverley Hillbillies'* kind of wave! If I were Sarah, I would have definitely turned around at that point and walked away ... double time!

But she didn't. What she did do was smile. It was a smile of curious bemusement rather than that of say, an old friend, but it was strangely warm nonetheless. And then, before I knew what I was doing, I'd begun to walk towards her.

"Hold on," George said, putting a hand on my shoulder and stopping me in my tracks. I turned to look at him and from the expression on his face, knew what he was about to say next before he actually said it. "This is something Ah huv tae do ma self, isn't it?" I smiled and nodded my head. He pondered for a second, glanced at Sarah and then took a deep breath. "Right. Wish me luck," he said softly. "God knows Ah need it!"

I held out my hand. "You'll be fine," I reassured him. "But good luck anyway!"

George paused for the slightest of moments and then took hold of my hand, not with one but with both of his own. He shook it gently and held on to it for a while. "Thank you," he began, sounding a little overwhelmed and choked. "Ah ... well Ah ..."

"I know," I said, nodding my understanding and sparing him from making a sentimental speech. I placed my free hand on top of his and smiled. I almost threw in a hug as well but I guessed that holding hands and looking knowingly into each other's eyes whilst standing on a busy street, was already probably more than George was comfortable with. "Now go and meet your daughter!" I simply instructed, as we released our grips.

He smiled and took a small step backwards. "Do Ah look ok?" he asked.

I looked him up and down and smiled. "Och aye son!" I replied and gave him a wink.

George rolled his eyes and tutted. "That accent still needs work," he said, bluntly. "But ye're getting there!" And with a wry smile and a wink of his own, he strode off towards a lady who was standing a mere five seconds away from a life-changing discovery.

I had watched George walk away on that day and speak to his daughter for the first time in his life. I had watched Sarah listening closely to whatever it was that he was saying and had seen her expression display a variety of emotions. I had seen her frown, nod, smile warily and then frown again. And I had watched with anxiety as the bombshell was finally dropped causing Sarah to throw her hands up towards her mouth in dumbfounded shock.

I saw tears, a dis-believing shake of the head, and a moment of rejection as Sarah stepped back slightly when George reached out and touched her arm. In those few tentative minutes, my stomach was on an emotional roller coaster and I wondered if talking George into this scenario had been the right thing to do.

George then stood in front of Sarah blocking my view and I suddenly had no way of telling how it was progressing. Was she going to walk away and reject him out of hand? Was she going to stay? Would she laugh, shout, scream, call the police?? I just didn't know. The suspense was killing me and I was contemplating walking over just to settle my own curiosity! But then I witnessed something that pushed that thought right out of my mind and caused me to sigh loudly with relief. For in what seemed to be a definite clearing of the first hurdle, Sarah's arms suddenly appeared around the back of George, pulling the big man towards her in a warm embrace. And as my breathing started to settle to an almost normal rhythm, I watched the bodies of two people tremble with emotion as they wept openly. To any other person on the street, this might have seemed a little distressing but to me, it was a moment of beauty. I had just witnessed the union of a father and his daughter for the first time in their lives and it felt good.

After a few more seconds of hugging, George held Sarah away at arm's length. From the smile and the nod of her head, it was obvious that her dad was saying something to her, though what it was, I couldn't say. What I can say, is how unexpected the next part of this scenario was.

George placed an arm around Sarah's shoulders and I watched the two of them begin to walk slowly away. I was in no doubt that they were off to find a quiet seat in a coffee house or restaurant or whatever, to start building on their new found relationship and though I wanted nothing more than the two of them to bond, I couldn't help but feel a little rejected. After all, I had spent many weeks getting to know George in a way that I am sure nobody else knew him and now, he was just walking away as if I hadn't existed. Don't get me wrong here. I knew that he had a little more on his mind than how I was

feeling and I understood that completely. It's just that ... oh I
don't know! Maybe I just wanted him to say goodbye or
something. In truth, the lack of acknowledgement put me on a
bit of a downer and though I can say, hand on heart, that it
wasn't jealousy I was feeling, it was pretty damn close!

But then, just as I was thinking about how they would
soon disappear into the lunchtime crowd and be gone, possibly
forever, George looked over his shoulder towards me and
offered up a casual but heart warming salute which
immediately lifted my mild depression. I should have
expected nothing less from the old Scot really and felt slightly
ashamed that I had. Nonetheless, I smiled widely, stood to
attention and returned the gesture with complete enthusiasm,
never more grateful for such a simple act.

At the point of our exchange, Sarah also glanced back,
no doubt curious as to what George was doing. She looked at
me for the second time that day, stopped walking and then
turned back to her father with an inquisitive look about her. I
saw her mouth move, forming the words *'who's that?'* just as
George began to lead her away again.

As my smile faded, I cast a glance up towards the dirty
grey sky, certain that the heavens were about to deliver yet
more rain and decided that it was also time for me to leave.
But as I looked back down onto street level, I saw that George
and Sarah had stopped walking again and were now holding
yet another conversation. I chuckled slightly, wondering if
they would actually make it to a coffee house before running
out of things to say. And then, as quickly as it had been
rekindled, the smile on my face faded once more as I watched
(with a little horror) Sarah holding up her hand to George in a
hang *on, I'll just be a minute, kind* of way and then start
heading back towards me. I suddenly felt a wave of
uneasiness wash over me as I began to panic, wondering what
it was she was going to say or do to me. Had I have had some
sort of pre-warning or indeed a little more time, I might have

even fled the scene. But she strode towards me with such speed and determination, I didn't have a moment to contemplate anything and just stood there with yet another supercilious grin on my reddening face.

"It's Paul isn't it?" she asked rhetorically, holding out her hand. When she spoke, her voice sounded mellow yet mildly commanding and carried only the slightest hint of a Scottish undertone. It was a voice designed to put people at complete ease ... a bit like a Doctor or that woman who's silky tones deliver directions to you via your sat-nav. And she was beautiful. My anxiety dissolved immediately. "I'm Sarah," she added.

I nodded and took hold of her hand that, despite the inclement weather, was exceptionally warm. "I know," I replied. "And it's a pleasure to finally meet you, Sarah!" And it really was. This lady had been a huge part of my conversations with George over the past few weeks and to actually see and then meet her in person was like finding the last missing piece of a jigsaw. Strangely, yet undeniably, satisfying!

"I just wanted to say hello and ..." She hesitated for the slightest of moments, smiled a wonderful smile and then moved closer towards me, hugging me and then kissing me on my cheek. When she pulled away, her smile was still in place though a noticeable glaze of tears had formed in her eyes. "Thank you!" she said softly. I could only nod and offer a smile of my own ... anything else would have ruined the moment.

She quickly made her way back to where George was standing and linked his arm as if it were the most natural thing in the world to do. And then I watched them walk slowly away until they were finally out of sight. If this had have been a movie, I thought to myself, then this would be the part where the music starts and the camera fades out ... And roll credits!

###

33

The day that I had watched George and Sarah walk off into a busy lunchtime crowd, I had a strangely overwhelming feeling that that would be the last time I ever saw them. It was a feeling that I was eager to suppress, if only to avoid the anticlimax that it would surely have brought with it. I didn't want that moment to be the finale of a bizarre yet interesting few months spent chatting with a stranger, because to me, George was no longer a stranger, he was a friend.

And so, I held on to the belief that our parting was more a *bon voyage* rather than a final goodbye and for three weeks following the reunion of father and daughter, I often ventured into the centre of Manchester expecting that I'd see George at one of our usual meeting places. Alas, my hopes, beliefs and expectations were gradually eroded away over that three-week period, as the elusive Scot was nowhere to be found. Sometimes, I would see and old down and out ambling along the street and race over with a childlike enthusiasm, only to discover, when I had gotten close enough, that it wasn't George. It did amaze me though, just how many seemingly homeless men over the age of fifty donned the streets of Manchester and I wondered if my time with George had in fact opened my eyes to an otherwise ignored problem? I couldn't decide whether this particular insight was a good or a bad thing but it certainly gave me a sense of perspective on my own fairly comfortable existence, which I had a tendency to take for granted. Maybe I should do more to help the less fortunate, I thought ... we'll see!

Anyway, where was I? ... Oh yes, the expectant search for George!

It was during one of my city centre visits (on yet another rain filled day) that my fading hopes were suddenly given a much-needed boost when I caught a glimpse of a familiar bright blue, polka dot umbrella from afar. I couldn't help but chuckle out loud as I watched it bobbing along the street and although I was unable to fully see the person under it, I could tell from the stature of the carrier that it was most definitely a male. It had to be George, I mused with growing excitement. I mean, what other man did I know would carry a lady's rain accessory with such conviction.

I walked hastily towards him, shouting out the old Scot's name as I navigated my way around other pedestrians. "George! ... George!" I shouted, wondering why my calling had absolutely no effect in making the man stop and respond. I decided to quicken my pace until I was just a few feet behind him and try again. "George!" A bit louder, still nothing.

When I did eventually manage to stop him (by literally jumping into his path) I was met with a cold and disgruntled stare from a totally unrecognisable face and I suddenly realised my stupid yet obvious mistake. In my quest to find George, I had hoped ... nay ... wanted this particular man to be him a great deal more, it would seem, than I had wanted to listen to my own subconscious telling me that it wasn't. My judgement had become more clouded than the winter sky of Manchester and though the bearer of the distinctive brolly was indeed a *gentleman of the road*, he wasn't mine.

In a futile attempt to limit my deserved embarrassment, I asked him how he had come about the umbrella hoping that it might at least give me a clue as to George's current whereabouts. However, the new owner was not what you would consider to be an affable soul and he looked me up and down with understandable suspicion. "I didn't steal it if that's what you're thinkin''?" he hissed.

"No, not at all!" I replied. "It's just ..."

"Good!" he intervened, sharply. "Now piss off and leave me alone!"

What a charming man!

And so it was, standing there in the middle of Manchester, watching Mr Rude saunter away under an icon of blue, that I finally came to accept the inevitable ... no matter how much I wanted it and no matter how long I cared to search, I wouldn't be seeing George again. The experience was over and if I didn't resign myself to that fact, I could find myself becoming obsessed with his whereabouts. I sighed and then shook my head, fighting the mild depression that was threatening to take hold. It wasn't easy, standing there in the rain wondering what to do next. But I knew one thing for sure. I needed to move on. I needed to pull myself together for God's sake!

And thankfully, by taking the positives of our time together, clinging onto them and drinking in the solace that they brought, I did. Yes, it was sad that George had gone but having had the opportunity to speak to him, I had gotten a great real life story that I could now look forward to telling. I had met my prejudices about the less fortunate street dwellers, head on and in the process, come to respect what a hard life most of them actually lead whilst gaining one of them as an unlikely friend. But more importantly, I had also helped bring a father and daughter together after so many years apart and that bit, dear readers, felt particularly good! In fact, I reckoned that that achievement called for a little celebration of my own ... and I knew exactly where I would indulge it.

34

The moody waitress placed my bacon sandwich and mug of thick looking tea in front of me. "Thanks," I said without a glance, presuming that, as usual, she would just mumble something unintelligible and move swiftly away. But this time she didn't. This time, she hovered at my tableside, causing me to look up at her with a slight frown.

"Where's your friend today?" she asked directly, taking me by complete surprise. Here was a question that would require a response, which, in short, was the start of an actual conversation. Not only was I surprised, I was a little touched that she had asked about George. There again, she had spoken out during our last visit to the cafe, advising George, in her own teenage style, that he needed to meet his daughter, so I guessed that had something to do with her inquiry. I also sensed a little awkwardness about her and put this down to her wanting to know the outcome of George's rendezvous without giving the impression that she was prying. It was quite endearing really, in its own way, so I decided to share what I knew, especially as she was clearly making the effort to be sociable.

"Starting a new life with his daughter I would imagine," I replied, smiling. "So I doubt we will see him again!" She sighed and I saw a distinct look of anguish on her face making me feel a little sorry for her. She must have secretly enjoyed having George and I as regular visitors and *overhearing* some of the tales he had to tell but I imagined she was either too shy or too cool to say so. Maybe she wasn't as hard-faced as she would have everyone believe? "I'm sure he's going to be ok though," I added, in the best comforting and reassuring tone that I could manage. "Although, it'll be a bit strange not having him around!" I smiled at her again, waiting for her to concur with my sentiments and tell me how she too thought it would be strange without George and how she was going to miss him and his unusual ways, now that he had gone. Was I right about her deep-seated feelings thus far? Had I finally gotten behind the armour of disdain and revealed a caring heart beneath? ... not even close Freud fans! For, in the words of the great man himself, it would seem that *a cigar really is just a cigar*!!

"Well," she began, with that same dis-interested glare that I had mistaken for genuine feeling. "I'm still owed money from when he was here with his daughter a few Thursdays ago!"

I frowned again, now slightly shocked. "What? He was in here? With his daughter? A few Thursdays ago?" I repeated, as though I were a parrot with mental health problems. "But that's the day that they met!" I said to her, though why I bothered to add this detail is beyond me, as she had absolutely no interest in what I was saying.

"Really? That's great!" she responded with more than a touch of sardonicism. "But he told me that you would settle his bill!"

"What?" I spluttered. "Me? ... settle *his* bill? ... he said that?" Same old parrot!

"Don't blame me. He's your mate!" She said bluntly before placing a three-week-old greasy bill on my table. "And this is what he had!" She was beginning to irritate me now.

"Oh yeah?" I began. "And how do I know that you just didn't forget to take his money?" You'd have thought that I had just insulted her mother, such was the look she gave me. It was as if her head was being operated by three fingers wedged into the back of it, like one of those spongy face puppets you can buy that display a grotesque expression when you squeeze your digits together.

"Er, I don't think so mate!" she spat, holding out her hands, palms up and recoiling slightly in that typical teenage *what you chattin'*? stance. "That's what he said. I'm not a liar!"

"Oh, so he said, 'don't worry that other man I usually come in with will pay' and you just accepted it?"

"More or less!" she replied.

"Whatever Trevor!" I can speak teenager too you know.

"And he told me to tell you something else if you didn't believe me!" she continued without faltering.

"Oh yeah?" I snorted. "Like what?" This I had to hear. What could she possibly pull out of the bag to convince me that her story wasn't a complete fabrication used in an attempt to recover her stupid oversight? She had backed herself into a corner and I was looking forward to watching her crumble ... bring it on!

And so it was, in less than thirty seconds, little Miss Attitude had left my table with a smug, supercilious smirk on her spotty face and payment in full for two English breakfasts (with extra toast), four large teas and two Eccles cakes to go. Twelve pounds and eighty pence, thank you very much. I don't know what stung more, the unexpected pay out or the public stoning of my pride? Deep down, I think I knew!

Still, as George had pointed out to the teen waitress a few weeks earlier, it was a lot cheaper than buying the bottle of Scotch that I owed him ... So I guess we were quits!

###

35

Despite the minor conflict with customer services, I stayed in the cafe for near on an hour whilst I reminisced about my time with George, recounting his tales of woe, hope, love and ghosts with a fondness that I would never have imagined possible. I was still amazed that the man I had set out to dismiss on day one had become such a significant part of my life over the previous months and I felt a new surge of shame that I had wrongly judged him and his circumstances merely from appearances. Would I do that again? There was every possibility but I certainly wouldn't rush into such a judgement without knowing at least some of the facts ... if nothing else, my experience with George had taught me that much! I raised my mug in a silent tribute to the Old Scot, wished him well in his new life and downed the final mouthful of lukewarm tea before heading out of the door.

I stepped out onto the footpath, thankful that the rain had finally ceased and took in a deep breath of cool air through my nostrils trying to clear the greasy smell that the cafe had bestowed upon them. And whilst I stood there deliberating over what to do next, a very bizarre thing happened. As if I had become some huge charitable magnet sucking in the needy, a man suddenly appeared at my side asking if I had any spare change. No, it wasn't George (sadly) but it was a homeless bloke with similar attire and I immediately knew what this unusual coincidence was all about ... it was a test! It had to be! Call it what you like, intuition, suspicion, destiny or just plain lunacy, I really felt like this scruffy little man had been positioned at this particular place, at this particular time to test me. Would I continue along the road of pre-judgement or would I follow through with my intention to change? Well, whatever you might think, it was actually the latter. I was about to embrace change better and quicker than a chameleon ... the new me had entered the building.

I smiled at the man, said nothing and put my hand into my pocket, digging deep for any coppers I could offer him. I tried the right and then the left pockets but then realised, with great dismay, that I'd actually used the last of my change paying for George's million-course meal. *'Shit!'* I thought. *'Now what?'* I was in a difficult situation. If I produced nothing, not only would his hopes of a little windfall be dashed but he would also think that I was lying about having no money. And although I could negate the latter by letting him search me, that was never going to happen in a month of sweet Sunday's was it?

Oh, I could've told him why I had no money, starting with the line, *you're never going to believe this,* but in reality, he probably wouldn't have.

'Bloody hell, what should I do?' I asked my inner self.

'Honesty is the best policy!' it replied.

"Have you got any change or what mate?" the homeless one asked again, becoming a little impatient. I realised that I only had one option left and if that was going to stop an increase in this man's agitation, then use it I must. Maybe honesty was the best policy?

And so, keeping my hands in my pocket, I stared at the needy male as warmly as I could and then told him exactly how it was.

"Ich spreche kein Englisch!" I delivered.

And ... shrug, smile a little and then shrug again.

Wait for a response? ... not this time folks, not this time.

DAS ENDE

Lightning Source UK Ltd.
Milton Keynes UK
UKHW01f0147090718
325417UK00001B/25/P